T0197299

The
Dance
Man

The Dance Man

STEPHEN HAYES

THE DANCE MAN

iUniverse books may be ordered through booksellers or by contacting:

iUniverse
1663 Liberty Drive
Bloomington, IN 47403
www.iuniverse.com
1-800-Authors (1-800-288-4677)

ISBN: 978-1-5320-5928-5 (sc)
ISBN: 978-1-5320-5930-8 (hc)
ISBN: 978-1-5320-5929-2 (e)

Library of Congress Control Number: 2018911856

Print information available on the last page.

iUniverse rev. date: 10/08/2018

For my Alabama cousins
Dick, Bill, Marian and Charlsie Jean

Chapter 1

MORT HAD JUST BROUGHT THE coffee mug to his lips when the bird slammed head-long into the kitchen window over the sink. Startled, he spilled his coffee onto his eggs and grits and into his lap. "Goddammit!"

"Please," Weenie said, "I've asked you a hundred times not to take the Lord's name in vain in my presence."

"And you, dear woman," Mort snarled, wiping coffee off the kitchen table, "have been asked a hundred times to do something to make that damned blackbird realize he can't join us in here for breakfast!"

"It's not a blackbird," Weenie said calmly. "I think maybe it's a grackle."

"Well, it's a damned stupid one. It's a kamikaze! I hope it has a headache. Better yet, a concussion."

Mort rose to refill his mug, returned to the small kitchen table and reached for the morning newspaper. He gazed for a moment out the side window, the one Kamikaze Karl had not yet attacked. It was a beautiful spring morning in Collier Bluff. The azaleas in the garden were in full bloom. The big yard sprawled south and west away from the house and sloped ever so gently toward the soft eastern bank of the river. The grass, which needed mowing, was a lush green. A gentle breeze ruffled the leaves of the giant magnolia tree that nestled against the weather-worn siding of the old house and swayed the Spanish Moss in the live oak trees.

As Mort turned to his weekly newspaper, the *Collier Caller*, there was a knock at the front door.

"I'll get it," Weenie said.

Mort listened to the big oak door creak open and an ensuing muffled conversation. His curiosity piqued, he went to the front hall and stood just behind Weenie who was talking to a pudgy, rosy-cheeked man dressed in khaki slacks, a white short sleeved shirt and necktie. The man peered behind Weenie and said, "Good morning, sir. I'm Charles Lodger, and I represent Face To Face Windows over in Mobile. I was just telling your wife here that—"

Mort stopped him. "She's not my wife, thank God. She's my sister. That's bad enough." He extended his hand. "I'm Mort Boozer."

"Nice to meet you. As I was saying—"

Weenie couldn't let the jab pass. "Yes," she chirped, "and this is my older—much older—brother, Mort. Mort is a nickname, short for mortified."

The salesman was at a loss for words.

"Yes," said Mort, also feigning cheeriness, "and I don't know if you were formally introduced to my kid sister, Weenie. Weenie, of course, is also a nickname. It refers to her teeny-weeny brain."

The salesman, by this time totally off his game, soldiered on. "Well, I can certainly see the family resemblance."

There was, in fact, a strong resemblance. Weenie and Mort both had rather thick, dark brown hair. Weenie's more salt and pepper than grey, Mort's heavier on the grey side. Mort stood a good half foot taller than his sister and a bit thicker in the waist. Weenie had kept herself quite trim through the years and, while not a beauty queen, was pleasant looking in a sporty, athletic sort of way. Both displayed the characteristic Boozer crows' feet around their blue eyes.

Lodger was saying, "I hope I'm not disturbing y'all. I just wanted to let you know that Face To Face carries a line of very high quality residential windows and—"

Mort interrupted the salesman again, "Face to face? That's the name of your company?"

"Oh, yes," Lodger said brightly. "Inspired, don't you think?"

"Inspired by what?"

"'For now we see through a glass darkly, but then face to face.' First Corinthians, Thirteen, Twelve. Inspired."

Bewildered, Mort stared face-to-face at Charles Lodger, asking finally, "You mean that with—"

"Oh, yes, sir!" Lodger exclaimed, "With our windows, you may look out at the world in a whole new way. Why you might even—"

Mort asked, "Are your windows warrantied against damage from demented blackbirds?"

"I told you it's not a blackbird," Weenie said.

"I'm sorry... demented ... what?" the salesman asked.

"Never mind," said Mort, stepping up next to his sister. "As you can see, Mister Lodger, this is an old house, and the window sizes are not standard."

"Oh, we can easily customize any order. "

"I'm sure you can, but we're really not in the market," Mort said.

Lodger took the rejection like a seasoned salesman. "Well, thank you for your time. If you know any neighbors that might be interested

"As a matter of fact," said Mort, "Mister Leland right across the way was just saying the other day he needed to replace all his windows."

"Really?" said Charles smiling broadly. "Why thank you."

"Good luck," Mort said, closing the door.

Weenie turned to her brother. "Why did you sic that poor man on Ellison, our nice neighbor?"

"Oh, it'll be good to infuse some human contact into Ell's otherwise dreary life."

Weenie sighed. "Yes, I guess you're right. I suppose one can't really consider the time he spends with you as human contact."

Mort couldn't think of a clever retort and simply stood for a moment in the middle of the foyer. Weenie went upstairs to dress for her morning meeting, although she couldn't remember if today was Bible study or the Collier Bluff Women's Bridge Club.

Mort called up to her, "See if Maggie's up, will you?"

Before Weenie could respond, a gravelly female voice called down from the second floor landing. "Yes, I'm up. Been up for hours. You got some coffee on down there?"

Mort looked up. "Yes, ma'am. Coffee's hot and fresh. So's the grits and eggs."

Maggie stared down at Mort. "I thought I heard the dance man a bit ago," she said. "You seen him this mornin'?"

"No, ma'am," Mort replied, "not today."

Maggie, attired in her frayed night gown, grunted, gripped the bannister with a gnarled hand and started her descent. Seymour, her longtime companion stood behind her, wagged his tail and followed her down. He was a hound of indeterminate breed, with short chocolate brown hair, long legs, silk smooth flopping ears, and only one functioning eye.

Chapter 2

OLLIER BLUFF, A SMALL TOWN in southwest Alabama, is nestled tight along the eastern bank of the Monacoosa River. When Mort was twelve, he left home for the first time, traveling by bus to spend part of August with his best friend, Henry, who had recently moved up to Atlanta. It was the summer of his first love, a tender puppy love romance with Lila Ann Sparks, an adolescent Georgia peach of a girl who was Henry's new next door neighbor. Back in Collier Bluff just before school began, the smitten young Boozer boy wrote to Lila Ann.

Sitting cross-legged on his bedroom floor, he finished the letter, read it over twice, folded it carefully and slid it into an envelope. As he licked the back flap of the envelope, a spontaneous welling up of goofy humor prompted him to write the following return address on the upper left hand corner:

Mort Boozer
Marsh Road
Call Your Bluff, Alabama

The new school year began and as the days drifted on, cooling ever so slightly, Mort waited with hidden longing for Lila's responding letter. It never came. *Did she really not like him? Did she have another boy friend? What was the problem?*

On an overcast day in November while walking to school, it suddenly dawned on him. "Oh, my god," he said out loud. "That's it!" She does love me, he thought, and she wrote back but the postman knew of no town called Call Your Bluff. *What an idiot!* Mort marched on to school, now with a spring in his step and a buoyant countenance, imagining a mailman with Lila Ann's perfumed love letter in hand, trudging through Alabama in search of Call Your Bluff.

Over the next few weeks, he thought many times of writing a second letter, but he never did. He also never mentioned his angst to his parents and would certainly not tell his sister about Lila Ann because he knew she would tease him unmercifully.

☙❧

The siblings' father, Mortimer Boozer, Senior, had married his high school sweetheart in the spring of 1941. By their first anniversary, he was in the Army, heading into the turbulent maw of World War Two. After the war, he returned to Collier Bluff to his bride and to a job at the local Rexall Drugstore. On September 4, 1946, Mr. and Mrs. Boozer were graced with a son whom they christened Mortimer Calhoun Boozer, Junior. Two years later, they welcomed Mort's little sister, Roweena Marian Boozer, into the world.

Mort and Weenie—the latter nickname came early and stuck hard—played together as children, but sparred and teased and fought as rival siblings are wont to do.

When Mort Junior entered his teen years, he began to change and not for the better. Maybe it was his first painful brush with love. Maybe it was the bursting flow of hormones. Or maybe it was the constant teasing at school. "Hey, Mort the dork." "How's it going, Mr. Mort, the mortician?" "Is everyone in your family a big boozer?" Mort became withdrawn, touchy, and sullen.

After some repetitive urging from his Mrs. Boozer, the father took his son out on the back porch one evening for *a little chat*. The back porch was, in fact, simply one side of a wide veranda that wrapped around the entire perimeter of the house. Heavy oak posts supported the large overhang which provided shade, shelter from the rain, and support for several hanging swing seats. They sat side-by-side in white wicker rocking chairs, creaking slowly back and forth, watching the fading December light.

"So, young man," Mort Senior began, still looking straight ahead, "Mom senses something's up with you. What's going on?"

Young Mort gazed straight ahead. "Nothin'."

"I think it's not nothing."

The boy looked down at his feet. "I dunno."

His father brought his rocker to a standstill. "The school says your grades are slipping. What's that all about?"

"I'll get 'em up."

They both stared in silence into the gathering night. Finally, the father said, "Weenie told me you got in a fight today."

Junior glared at his father. "She told you that? I'm going to strangle that little—"

"You're not going to strangle anyone. Now you tell me, young man, what was the fight about?"

Junior craned his head and stared at the porch ceiling. He spoke slowly. "Do you have any idea what it's like to go to school every day carrying a name like Mortimer Boozer?"

"Actually," the father said, "I do have an idea because—"

Junior was not listening. "It is really crap," he interjected. "I just wish I could have a better name. I also wish I could get the hell out of this crummy hick town."

"I'll tell you this, young man," father admonished, "I can't help you with your given name. But you keep up your bad grades and ornery behavior, and you just might get your second wish. You better straighten up and quick!"

෨෦෨

Three months later, after another testy talk on the back porch, Mort's second wish, in fact, did come true. On a drizzly winter morning, the two Mortimer Boozers left Collier Bluff at dawn in the family's 1953

Chevrolet. They arrived long after dark in the Shenandoah Valley town of Staunton, Virginia, found an inexpensive motel room, and fell exhausted into a hard sleep onto a soft bed.

The next morning, by previous appointment, they were seated in front of a large antique desk, the desk of the commanding officer of the venerable Staunton Military Academy.

Colonel Thomas Ragsdale was a sturdy sort. Steely blue eyes. Bushy red-brown eye brows and a bushier drooping mustache. Ruddy pock marked cheeks. The colonel spoke, "Welcome to the Academy, gentlemen. I trust the drive was not too arduous."

"Not bad," Mort Senior said. "long, but not too bad." The father was now having second thoughts about his decision to send his son away to school. He said, "I got your letter about our appointment."

"Yes. That is apparent, since you are both here," the colonel said.

Junior rolled his eyes while his father stumbled on. "And I appreciate the fact that you are willing to enroll Mort in the middle of the school year."

"Yes. It's not common practice," the colonel said, "but I inferred from your letters that you were, well, a bit in extremis, shall we say?"

Father Boozer and the headmaster talked on for a few minutes while Mort Junior looked absently around the big office and occasionally up at the ceiling.

"So I think we are all set then," Colonel Ragsdale said finally. "Rest assured. You've brought him to the right place. We will get him squared away. Don't worry."

Mort had no idea what *squared away* meant, and he wasn't real sure he wanted to know.

The meeting was over. They all stood. Mort Senior wanted to hug his son, but thought better of it. They shook hands while the father said, "Do your best here, son. I'll come get you at the end of the school year."

Mort's father shook the headmaster's hand and departed.

Colonel Ragsdale moved behind the massive desk and gestured with an open palm. "Have a seat, young man."

Mort turned, looking out the window just in time to see his father drive down the campus lane toward the academy front gate. He sat down and faced El Commandante Mal, a term he would soon learn all cadets used behind the colonel's back.

"Mort," the colonel began, "after today you will always be referred to as Mister Boozer. But today, just today, I will call you Mort."

"Okay," Mort said flatly.

"And after today, you will address me at all times as Colonel or Sir. And you will address all other senior officers accordingly."

"Okay. I mean yes, sir," Mort said.

Colonel Ragsdale slowly paged through the open folder in front of him. Still looking down, he said, "Mortimer is a rather unusual name. Not really a Southern name, is it?"

On the long drive up to Virginia, Mort had pondered yet again his hated name and had concocted a strategy for just such an occasion. It was an opportunity, he hoped, to start anew. "Yes," he said brightly. "It's a family name. But nobody calls me Mort at home."

The colonel stared at the boy for a moment. "You meant to say 'yes, sir,' I'm sure."

"Uhh, yes, sir," Mort stammered.

"Your father called you Mort."

"I know, but he doesn't count," Mort said.

"I gather," the colonel said dryly. He studied his new recruit for a minute, and then asked, "What do folks call you back home?"

Mort had prepared himself for the question. "Lance," he said proudly, quickly adding, "Sir."

The colonel's bushy eye brows arched and his eyes widened. "Lance?"

"Yes, sir. It's a nickname."

"Of course." The colonel looked back down at the folder. "Lance is a common nickname for Mortimer."

Mort missed the sarcasm. The colonel looked pensively out the window for a long time, slowly twisting one of his mustache handle bars with thumb and index finger. Finally, he turned to his new charge and said, "Well, let me tell you, Lance, about our academy, what our goals and methods are, and what will be expected of you."

And so began the daunting challenge, daunting and agonizing to all involved, of getting Mortimer Calhoun Boozer, Junior squared away.

Now some forty-five years later, Mort, who never quite got himself squared away, watched Aunt Maggie shuffle toward the head of the dining room table, a table that had been in the family for a hundred years. The table had been handcrafted long before the Civil War, the war folks around Collier Bluff, of course, referred to as the "War of Northern Aggression."

Auntie was a bit unsteady on her feet and reached for the edge of the big table. Mort remained seated, knowing not to offer any assistance. He knew from hard experience she would swat him away and scold, "Le'me be, young man. Ah ain't a cripple!" So Mort was always careful to stay out of her line of fire. Having just turned fifty-seven, he smiled faintly at the thought of anyone calling him *young man*.

She stoically inserted herself between the table and the chair and lowered her rump into her seat. Seymour, her four-legged companion, padded under the table and quietly took his customary position resting his head on Maggie's feet.

Weenie called from the kitchen, "Maggie, you want some grits or a soft boiled egg?"

Auntie chided over her shoulder, "Girl, you been livin' here some time now. You know what I want. Coffee with milk." She hesitated a moment, then added, "Maybe some tomata juice."

The old lady turned her head and stared out at her side garden through her thick bottle-bottom glasses. Except for the metronomic ticking of the grandfather clock in the hall, the house was quiet. She blinked, then still gazing out the window, said to Mort, "I thought you were goin' to fix that bench out there for me."

"Yes, ma'am, I am. I gotta get a new pine board. A nice straight one. Just haven't got to it yet."

"Yes, I know," Maggie graveled with thinly veiled sarcasm. "I know how terribly busy you must be." Then she abruptly announced, "Gotta take a pee. Be right back." She put both hands flat on the table and struggled, slowly straining to push herself upright.

Mort waited for her to shuffle out to the hall and around the corner, then turned to his sister, who had come into the room. "She pays Jonah for work around here. Why can't he fix the bench?"

"He's away, remember?" Weenie said. "He and Eugenia went over to Jackson."

"When's he comin' back?"

"I don't know, and I think you'd best forget about Jonah and get on with that bench."

Mort slurped his coffee. "By the way," he said, "what is the deal with Maggie always muttering about a dance man? What is she talking about?"

"I haven't the slightest idea," Weenie said absently.

Maggie slowly walked back into the dining room and repeated her arduous descent into her chair.

Chapter 3

M AGGIE, CHRISTENED MAGNOLIA DABNEY BOOZER, was born three years before her brother, Mortimer Senior, came into the world. She and Mort Senior were the grandchildren of Gustav Bhuser, the first Bhuser, later converted to Boozer, to settle in Alabama. Gustav, who quickly became known as Gus when he came to the United States, hailed from a long line of shipping merchants in the Old Country. Like so many European immigrants at the time, he first set foot on American soil in New York and tried to build a new life there. But in less than a year, he became discouraged and wanted to escape the rough and tumble life in Brooklyn. He heard of trading opportunities in another shipping port. A port in the south somewhere. A port called Mobile. So the émigré packed his meager belongings and headed south on foot. With exquisite and very unfortunate timing, Gus arrived in Alabama just two days before the Union Admiral Farragut blockaded the port of Mobile from all shipping.

Abandoning his shipping ambition, Gus scrambled his way through several lines of business, succeeding well enough over the years to marry, support a family and eventually purchase the handsome, but rather decrepit home on Marsh Road on the outskirts of Collier Bluff. Maggie, known in her early years as Magnolia, was a very young woman, barely out of her teens, when Grandfather Gus died suddenly and left the house and grounds to her.

The antebellum house was a wooden structure with high ceiling rooms, multiple fireplaces and an expansive front veranda, a stately, if rather faded, grey specimen of the Old South. Some folks referred to the old home as the "Gray Lady along the Monacoosa." Behind the kitchen, a dense tangle of Scuppernong grape vines had wrapped themselves around a back door portico post, across the frontal piece over the door, and back down the second post. Over the years, Maggie had let Jonah, the yard man, harvest the grapes in the fall for jelly or, in some years, for homemade Scuppernong wine.

☙❧

The current familial living arrangement began shortly after Weenie finally divorced Roy Sweeney, leaving him in Little Rock, Arkansas, with his only friend, Jim Beam, and moved back home to Collier Bluff. Wanting no association with "that slug of a man," she changed her last name back to Boozer. The name change carried the added benefit of no longer having to endure life as Weenie Sweeney.

Earlier that same year, Randy Lee Paxton, Maggie's husband of almost sixty years, was driving home from the grocery store and plowed straight into the largest, oldest and most revered magnolia tree in town. The magnificent specimen stood close by Marsh Road, along the river, right beyond a big bend. No one really knew what caused the smash up except that it resulted in a quick end to Randy Lee. Some folks in town quietly joked that "ol' Mister Paxton maybe jus' ran into Magnolia one too many times."

As a youngster, Weenie had always been close to her aunt. After Uncle Randy Lee's demise, she fretted that her aunt would not be able to manage alone and offered to move in with her in the big house. The fact that Weenie, having recently relocated back to town, had little money, no job and no real place to stay, was presumably not related to her concern for her widowed aunt.

Mort Senior, upon his passing, had left both Weenie and Mort Junior a small monthly stipend for life. The stipend was too small to live on, but large enough to acquire basic necessities. It was also large enough, at least in Junior's case, to keep any robust drive or ambition in check.

A month or so after Randy Lee was laid to rest, Mort Junior developed his own *deep concern for poor Aunt Maggie* and also graciously offered to move in *just temporarily* to help her out.

One chilly night while sitting by the fire with her ever present bourbon on the rocks, Maggie allowed as how "it would indeed be helpful to me if you two could stay for a bit to help me get settled without Randy Lee." And that, then, was how it all started.

ᑫᑫᑫ

Weenie pushed open the swinging kitchen door with her rump and rotated into the dining room, tray in hand. She lovingly bent over Maggie and carefully placed a cup of coffee with milk and a glass of tomato juice in front of her. She said, "Maggie, you need to put some meat on your bones, hon. Are you sure you won't eat a soft boiled egg? Or maybe some toast?"

Maggie reached for her coffee. The cup quivered unsteadily as she cradled it in both hands and brought it to her lips. She took a slurping sip and turned ever so slightly back toward Weenie. "No, thank you. No heavy meals. I don't want to burden my pall bearers."

Mort chuckled.

"Hush now with such talk," Weenie admonished. "The last thing you need to worry about is your pall bearers."

Maggie placed both hands on the table again. "Well," she began, "I was just thinkin'—"

Her thought, whatever it was, was punctured by a sudden bang against the side of the house. Even with her failing hearing, Maggie heard it and looked up in time to see a boy run past the window. She struggled to get to her feet. "Those damned kids!" she growled. "They've got no respect." She gave up the struggle to stand and turned her angry gaze toward her nephew. "They're trespassing on private property, those hooligans! Please get them out of here now or I'll call—"

"Maggie," Mort raised an open palm hand, a plea to calm down. "They're just young boys."

"Off!" she snapped. "Get them off my land!"

"Yes, ma'am." Mort was already heading to the front door.

In the side yard, he was shouting as loudly as he could, hoping Maggie could hear him. "Hey, you rapscallions! Don't you ever throw that ball over here again. Just get on!"

The scolding died down and more muted discussion ensued that Maggie could not hear and of which Weenie could only catch pieces. "We're really sorry, Mister Boozer…an accident…okay, boys…she's very…just don't…," and finally Mort's voice, now louder again for Maggie's benefit, "Alright now. Here's your ball. Now you head on home!"

Mort returned to the dining room, sat and pulled himself back up to his half eaten breakfast. He looked over at his aunt and said, "I really put the fear of the Lord into those boys."

Maggie's recall of the past few minutes had floated off into the humid Alabama air. She looked blankly at Mort. "You did what?"

Mort rolled his eyes.

"It's nothing," Weenie said kindly, then shifted gears. "I do wish you would eat something. I have a ripe grapefruit I just bought yesterday and some bran muffins."

Maggie turned her head, looked out through her thick bottle-bottom glasses and said, "No thank you. I'm still workin' on my coffee."

Weenie sighed.

Mort cut his last sausage link into thirds, reached for the plastic bottle of Aunt Jemima Syrup, and said, "I think those boys are going to bring you some flowers to apologize."

"What boys?" Maggie asked.

Mort and Weenie exchanged glances. Mort popped a piece of sausage in his mouth and looked over at the old lady. Still chewing, he spoke. "Maggie, I've always been curious why you and Uncle Randy Lee never had any children."

Auntie stared into empty space for a long time, trying, it seemed, to remember. She took a sip of coffee and dabbed her lips with her white paper napkin. "Well," she started, "I guess part of it was 'cause of my brother."

"Your brother?" Weenie asked.

"Yes. I remember Morty had these two kids. A boy and a girl. They were a royal pain in the you-know-what." She looked back into that empty space. "'Specially the boy. God, he was a mess. Raising hell all the time. Disrespectful. I think Morty finally had enough. Sent the little urchin to an army school somewhere up north. The girl was a mess, too." Maggie paused and took a deep breath. "So Randy and I just sorta decided we didn't want to get into all that."

Weenie and Mort, mouths open, stared wide-eyed at one another.

"Yep," Maggie rasped, "that's kinda what I remember. Wonder what ever happened to those little ruffians?" She looked into her empty coffee cup. "I'm gonna go get dressed and get started on the day," she said. "Maybe check in with the dance man." She began her slow, laborious process of standing.

Like Mort, Weenie knew from painful experience not to help her. She and her brother watched in silence, sipping their own coffee.

Maggie shuffled into the front hall toward the stairs with her faithful canine companion close behind. Seymour looked warily back at Mort before turning into the front foyer. When Mort first moved into the house, he had found Seymour's ugly blind eye, with its half-opened blood shot eye ball surrounded by gnarled scar tissue, hard to look at. One day on impulse, when the ladies of the house were away, he cut a rectangle of duct tape and stuck it over the dog's bad eye. The tape drove poor Seymour crazy until Mort took pity on him and ripped it off amidst much yelping and whining. Since that day, Seymour was always wary of Mort and gave him a wide berth.

Weenie stood to clear the table. Plate in one hand, coffee mug in the other, Mort quickly followed his sister into the kitchen. He put his mug and dish into the sink and leaned in to Weenie. "What the hell was that?" he asked. "Did you hear her in there?"

"I heard alright," Weenie said. She arched her head to the ceiling and closed her eyes. Mort couldn't tell if it was a gesture of exasperation or a plea to her god for deliverance. Maybe both. With her eyes still closed, she said, "She's really losing it, poor dear."

"Poor dear!" Mort was getting more agitated. "Poor dear? She went on about those bratty kids. Weenie, those kids is us!"

"Those kids are us."

"I really don't need a grammar lesson right now," Mort complained. "This is serious. We're living right under her nose and all this time she doesn't even know who we are!"

Weenie started in on the dishes. "She thinks that way about two kids she remembers from fifty years ago. I think its great news that she doesn't know it's us. Let's just leave it that way."

Mort retrieved his coffee mug from the sink and pondered what Weenie had said. A sudden loud thwack cracked behind him causing him to spill coffee all down his front. "Goddammit!" Mort turned angrily toward the kitchen window.

"Mort, please!"

"I'm gonna kill that friggin' bird!"

"Will you relax? A couple more attacks and it'll kill itself."

Mort wiped the front of his shirt with a paper towel and returned to matters at hand. "What are we going to do about Maggie?"

"Do? We're not going to do anything," Weenie said. "In case you haven't noticed, she's not real fond of you. What do you think she would be like if she figured out who you are—I mean *were*?"

"Yeah, I guess," Mort replied.

Weenie wiped her hands with a dish towel. "Why don't you change your shirt and go fix the bench?"

Mort was still looking for the demon aviary.

"Oh wait," Weenie said, "can you finish up here? I forgot I'm going to be late for Bible study."

"Okay," Mort said, turning his attention to the sink. "Study hard. When's the exam?"

Weenie, unsmiling, jutted her chin. "That line was slightly amusing the first hundred times you used it. We will never stop studying."

"Yeah. You know why? Because the Bible is a whopping pile of complications, contradictions, and weird anomalies."

"Wow!" Weenie said. "Pretty fancy words for a guy who never went to college." She added, "Why don't you come sometime? It wouldn't kill you."

Mort ignored the invitation and rinsed his mug. "Is the test multiple choice or essay?"

"I've got to get going," Weenie snapped. "But for your information, the test is an in-person oral exam given by Saint Peter. But where you're going, I'm sure you won't have to worry about it."

Chapter 4

THE ORIGINAL FIRST BAPTIST CHURCH of Collier Bluff burned to the ground shortly after the Civil War. The second First Baptist Church, built on the same site a block off the main square in town, was a white clapboard structure with a soaring cross-topped steeple. Two large Crepe Myrtle trees shouldered themselves on either side of the front door.

Over the years, most of the Boozer clan had attended the First Baptist Church of Collier Bluff. Mother Boozer started early with her kids, enrolling each into Sunday school when they turned four. Mort seemed to enjoy it, at least at first. But it wasn't too long before he tired of crayoning pictures of donkeys and men in robes with black beards. Luke Betterly, an older boy in the Sunday school class, taught Mort about spit balls and Scotch taping girls pig tails together. So it wasn't that Mort didn't like the teachings or the songs. It was just that he was introduced to other activities that were more interesting and more fun. But when he was seven or so, his attitude toward the Christian faith turned from benign indifference to subtle hostility. Oddly, it was not the theology itself that was the problem. Brother and sister had developed a healthy, perhaps all too healthy, sibling rivalry. Mort delighted in tormenting his younger sister and she, in defense, developed ever more devious ways to exact revenge.

Roweena, in contrast to her brother, took to Sunday school immediately and at family dinners she was always anxious to share her Sunday school stories and songs. Mort, responding to stimulus like Pavlov's dog, turned against anything his sister liked. He especially enjoyed teaching little sister about the wonderful old hymn, "Gladly The Cross I'd Bear", telling her it was about a cross-eyed grizzly bear named Gladly. He continued to go to Sunday school because he had no choice, but from the back seat of the family car, he repeatedly demanded to know why he had to go "to the First Baddest Church" in town.

And so began the tiresome theological tit-for-tat between brother and sister that had been continuing now, with varying degrees of acrimony and intensity, for more than half a century.

୧୨

Aunt Maggie had gone upstairs, as she always said, to "get dressed and start my day." But almost always something apparently came over her in her room and she would wind up back in bed. Usually she would reappear, still in her night gown and bathrobe, around lunch time to try again to start her still unstarted day.

Mort finished the dishes and stood guard for a while at the back window in wait for his winged nemesis. He soon tired of the vigil and, with an uncharacteristic display of initiative, headed out the back door. He plucked a handful of Scuppernong grapes from the vine, popped them in his mouth and drove to the local lumber yard.

For two days he worked steadily rebuilding the old garden bench. He cut and sanded and nailed a solid new seat board into place. He replaced six of the back rest slats and sanded smooth the arm rests. On the morning of the third day, he knelt in the garden before his masterpiece, and with a large screw driver opened a newly purchased can of gleaming white paint. He slowly began to paint both the old and new pine. Mort was on his knees working on the front legs of the bench when a voice from behind startled him. "That's a mighty fine piece of work there, Mister Boozer."

He turned with a jerk. It was Jonah coming around the garage. "Hey there," Mort said. "When d'you get back?"

"Last night."

"Good trip?"

"Not so good. Genia's sister passed. But we got to see her and be with her for a while."

"I'm sorry to hear. Please tell Genia we send our condolences."

Jonah had done yard work and odd jobs around the old house as long as anyone could remember. Mort regarded him kindly and wondered, as he had so many times before, how old the man was. No one, including Jonah, seemed to know for sure. He was taller than Mort, a lanky sort. His short cropped hair under his ever present straw hat was all grey. His large hands were cracked and calloused. His face was wrinkled, but when he smiled he showed off the whitest, prettiest row of teeth Mort had ever seen. Teeth that, perhaps because they were surrounded by such black skin, seemed so bright.

Weenie opened the back screen door and leaned out. "Mort, it's five of ten."

"Just a minute. I'm almost finished."

"No! I've got to go now. You promised," Weenie said sharply.

Mort turned to Jonah. "I've got to drive her out to church, but this….."

Jonah stopped him with an outstretched hand. "Give me the brush, Mister Boozer. I'll finish up here for you."

"Oh that would be a big help. I'll be back just in a bit."

Mort deposited his sister "at the First Baddest Church"—alternatively referred to by Mort as the First Battiest Church—for her committee meeting. It was an ad hoc committee formed to discuss the advisability of procuring multiple sets of spring vestments for the minister that would match the predominant color of azaleas in bloom in the courtyard each month. It would be a very long meeting.

Mort drove back to the house and pulled into the driveway. Walking toward the garage, he heard voices in the backyard. He stepped quietly just around the corner and stood unobserved. Maggie, barefoot and in her bathrobe, was standing under the old magnolia tree next to Jonah who was holding a paint can in one hand and a brush in the other. Seymour lingered idly by Maggie's side searching with his one eye for something to chase.

"Jonah, bless your heart," Maggie was saying as she admired the bench. "I've been after that fellow livin' here. That man—"

"Mort?" Jonah asked.

"Yes. That's him, Mort. Has the same name as my late brother. He kept sayin' he was going to fix the bench, but he's never lifted a damn finger."

Jonah placed the open can on the grass and laid the paint brush across its top. "Miss Maggie," he said, "Mister Mort here fixed the bench for you. I just got back from Jackson last night. I'm just helping him finish up."

Maggie was now confused, even more so than normal. She looked at the bright, white bench then back at Jonah. "But I just came out here, and you were doin' the bench. 'Sides, Mort could'na done that good a job."

Mort walked into the yard. "Mornin', Auntie. Good to see you up and around."

Maggie turned. "Hello," she said without expression.

Mort decided not to risk a fight. "Jonah, you sure have done a fine job with that bench."

"Mister Boozer, I tried to tell her—"

Mort and Jonah turned to one another and talked in a low voice. Maggie's ever diminishing attention span drifted elsewhere. She stepped over to her new bench and slowly lowered her self onto the wet paint.

Chapter 5

THE HOUSE WAS QUIET. GOLDEN afternoon sunlight shafted through the front window. Seymour was sprawled on the faded, blue and yellow braided rug in the center of the room. A nineteenth century mahogany hutch in the corner served as the house bar. Paint peeled overhead on the high ceiling. Mort and Weenie sat in the living room on the two wing chairs by the fire place. Weenie pulled on a loose thread on her arm rest. "Why don't we have a fire?" she asked. "It'd be cozy."

Mort looked at her. "A fire? It's the middle of May."

Weenie absent-mindedly gazed out the window. "Well, let's at least have a drink. We don't need to wait for Maggie."

"Capital idea." Mort walked to the side board. "I think I'll have a bourbon."

"You'd better not," Weenie said. "You'll catch hell."

"She won't remember."

"That's her bourbon. You know she's very possessive about it. I wouldn't chance it."

Mort pouted. "Oh, alright." He poured two glasses of red wine, sat down and raised his glass. "Cheers."

"Cheers."

Mort sipped his wine. "I wonder what's up with Maggie. Not like her not to be down for happy hour."

"Who knows," Weenie said, staring outside, listening to the faint tick-tocking of the grandfather clock in the hall. Finally, Weenie spoke again, "Dabney called this morning."

"Oh, what does she want now?" Mort asked dryly.

"She didn't want anything," Weenie said, visibly irritated. "Please stop it with the snide stuff."

"The snide stuff? You're the one who's always calling her Ditzy Dabney and Daffy Dabney."

"Well, I'm her mother," Weenie snapped, "and I can call her anything I want. But you should show respect."

Mort took another sip, actually kind of a gulp. "Sorry, but that daughter of yours is almost thirty now and—"

Weenie cut him off. "Look, I'm doing the best I can. You've never been a parent, so I don't need any lectures from you about Dabney." She took a deep breath, adding quietly, "And for your information, she's thirty-two."

Mort was now feeling contrite. "I'm sorry you're having a hard time with her."

Weenie closed her eyes, her tone softer. "Mort, I wish you and Marcie had gotten married. Maybe had kids. Dabney would have had some cousins. Would've been nice."

"Yep. It would've," Mort agreed, looking pensively down at his drink.

Weenie regarded him for a long time. "I never understood what happened with you two. You seemed so close."

After Mort struggled and floundered for a year and a half at Staunton Military Academy, his father, finally throwing in the towel, had brought him back home and enrolled him in Collier Bluff High School. That is where young Mort met Marcie Pelham and where they became sweethearts.

"To tell you the truth," Mort said, "I'm not so sure myself what happened. It was all kind of weird."

Weenie leaned toward her brother. "Kind of weird? How?"

Mort took a long draw on his drink, drained the glass, and walked to the sideboard for a refill. As he poured, his back to Weenie, he answered her, "The summer after high school, we were together all the time. In the fall, she went up to South Carolina for college. We wrote all the time. Saw

26

her on holidays. The next summer was great. We were together, really hot and heavy. Almost like we were married already."

He stared, turned around seemingly mesmerized and stared at the fading block of sunlight on the carpet at his feet.

Weenie nudged, "So then?"

Mort blinked and returned to his chair. "So then, she goes back to Limestone College for her second year. After a while, I don't get so many letters, and the ones I get seem a little different somehow." Mort filled his cheeks and exhaled heavily. Weenie waits. "Later that fall, right when she was supposed to come home for Thanksgiving, I get this letter. She says her Dad has been transferred to St. Louis and she's transferring to a college out there and that she'll write to me when she gets settled."

Weenie was now leaning even further forward, elbows on her knees, her wine glass cradled in both hands.

"Did she?"

"Nope. Never heard from her."

"That makes no sense."

"The really strange part," Mort said, "is that I went to her house, you know over on Brownfield Road. There was a For Sale sign in the front yard and the house was totally empty." Mort drank more wine. "I wrote her some letters to Limestone and asked that they be forwarded to her. Never heard back."

"Wow! You never told me all that."

"No, I guess I didn't. I just couldn't understand any of it. Took me a long time to get over it, I can tell you that." Mort slumped back in his chair.

"What a sad story," Weenie said. "I remember you really liked her and I thought she was crazy about you."

"Yep. Maybe. Or maybe just crazy." Mort sighed.

They were both quiet for a long time. Weenie, seeming to break out of her own trance, said, "Would you go up and check on Maggie? It's really not like her not to be down for happy hour."

Mort placed his glass on the sideboard and went upstairs. A minute passed, after which he called down, "She's not here!"

"What!" Weenie raced to the second floor and into the master bedroom sputtering, "Oh, my God! Oh, my God!" She stared at Maggie's big high posted bed, and then quickly got down on her knees to peer under the bed.

Mort, standing in the doorway, said, "Weenie, I've looked everywhere."

Weenie, now frantic, ignored him. She opened the bedroom closet and pushed the hanging clothes from side to side and looked into the back of the closet. She backed out of the closet, her eyes darting around the room. She went over to the big dresser and proceeded to open each drawer.

"Sis," Mort said, "I'm pretty sure she's not in the dresser."

Weenie spun around. "Mort, this is serious!"

Mort walked to her, placed his hand under her elbow and guided her gently to the settee by the window. "Let's sit for a minute and think," he said.

Weenie sat, her worried eyes still darting around the room, searching.

"Now, let's reconstruct," Mort said. "We had lunch together around one. You cleaned up, and Maggie said she was going upstairs to 'do some work' which, of course, meant she was going back to bed."

"Right," Weenie added, "and you went to the store and—"

"And I stopped to check in with Jimmy," Mort said.

"And later, Alice picked me up and we went to the hospital to see Mavis."

Mort took a deep breath. "I just can't figure."

Weenie looked at the rotating fan overhead. She closed her eyes. "I think we should call the police."

Before Mort could decide what he thought of the idea, Weenie was heading down stairs. She reached the foyer and turned left toward the old black telephone that sat on a small back hall table.

Then, from behind her, she heard the familiar scratchy voice. "There you are. I 'bin waitin' for ya."

Weenie froze in her tracks. She turned slowly to see Maggie sitting in her customary chair in the living room. She rushed toward her. "Oh, Maggie, we have been so worried about you. Where've you been?"

Maggie looked at Weenie through her thick glasses and scolded, "Where have I been? Where have you been? It's cocktail time. I 'bin sittin' here. Had to pour my own bourbon." She sniffed. "A lady shouldn't have to make her own drink."

Mort came in to the living room. Looking up at him and pointing a gnarled finger Maggie said, "That fella usually makes my bourbon for me."

"That fella?" Weenie said, "You know who he is, don't you?"

"Of course, I know who he is."

Weenie knew she didn't know, but said anyway, "I know you know." She plopped in her customary chair by the fireplace. "Maggie, Mort and I were here in this room for almost an hour waiting for you to come down and join us."

"Come down from where?" Maggie asked.

"We thought you were up in your room."

"I wasn't in my room."

"We know that."

"Then why did you think I was in my room?"

Weenie took a deep breath, while Mort struggled to suppress a laugh. "I mean we know now," Weenie said, "but we didn't know at first."

"Well, if you had just come in here for cocktail time like you're s'posed to, I could have told you." Maggie's mention of cocktail apparently reminded her that she had one in her hand. She took a healthy swig and said, "Well, you're both late, come on now and pour yourselves a tall one."

The siblings, fresh drinks in hand, settled in. Weenie put her glass on the ottoman in front of her, placed her hands on her knees and braced herself for another go around with the old lady. "Now, Maggie, I'd like to ask you a question."

"Fire away," Auntie said breezily.

"Okay. Do you remember where you were right before you came in here?"

Maggie puzzled over the question. "Right before?"

"Yes. Right before."

"Well." Maggie thought for a moment. She looked over her shoulder and pointed to the foyer. "Well, right before I came in here, I was there. In the hall."

Weenie closed her eyes. Mort laughed. Maggie glared at Mort, but said nothing.

Mort whispered to Weenie, "Give it up, Sis. It is what it is. Whatever it was."

The three sat and sipped in silence, after which Maggie suddenly said, "Rosie picked me up this afternoon. We had a nice ride."

Rosie Jamison was Maggie's niece on Roy Lee's side of the family. In recent weeks, Maggie had ventured out on several mysterious "rides with Rosie." Not always, but on more than one occasion – like today – she would quietly slip away and return home unseen.

"Oh, that sounds very nice, Maggie," Mort said. "Where did you two go?"

Maggie looked up at the high ceiling, thinking. She said, finally, "Oh, you know. Just thither and yon."

"Interesting," Mort said, feigning serious interest. "Which did you like better?"

"Which what?"

"The thither or the yon," Mort said. "Did you have a favorite?"

"Mort, knock it off!" Weenie snapped.

Maggie looked at Mort. "Young man, you are making no sense. Were you drinking before we started drinking?"

"Oh, no ma'am," Mort lied convincingly.

Weenie returned to her original line of questioning. "Maggie, you and Rose Ellen go out together a lot, but we never know where you go."

Maggie drained the last of her bourbon. "That's right," she said, and that was all she said. She turned to Mort and rattled her ice cubes. "I'll have another, if you don't mind."

Chapter 6

MORT WAS SITTING ON MAGGIE's bench in the back garden. In fact, his derriere was covering the famous sitzmark made in the paint by Maggie's derriere several weeks prior. It was a spectacular Alabama morning. The sky was blue, the sun was shining, and a gentle breeze off the river swayed the Spanish moss in the live oak trees. Steam wafted from his favorite University of Alabama Roll Tide coffee mug. Mort had not darkened the door of the University of Alabama, nor any school of higher learning for that matter. But he was fiercely loyal to the Crimson Tide of the university and to their football team. Reading the just delivered weekly edition of the *Collier Current*, he sipped his coffee and lazily snacked on a small pile of grapes lying on the bench by his side. He glanced overhead through the branches of the magnolia tree. Not a cloud in the sky. —What a day, he thought, what a wonderful day to be alive in L.A.—Lower Alabama.

His reverie was broken by the creaking of the kitchen screen door. Weenie poked her head out. "See you later. I'm off to Bible study."

"Okay."

Weenie paused to look more closely. "Mortimer, are those Maggie's grapes you've got there?"

"Uhh....."

"How many times do I have to remind you they are for Jonah and Genia. Now, stop pickin''em!"

"Yes, ma'am." Mort popped a grape into his mouth.

Weenie disappeared, then opened the door again and said, "By the way, what is this on the window here?"

"What?" Mort asked.

"On the window with suction cups. It's a bird feeder," Weenie said.

"Well, if you know what it is, then why did you ask?"

"I know what it is," Weenie said, "but it's on the inside."

Mort patiently folded his newspaper, giving Weenie his full attention. "That is correct," he said calmly. "I'm luring that little kamikaze bastard into the window."

"Well, as we have seen, he's very capable of hitting the window without a lure," Weenie said.

"Ah, yes, but this will hasten his demise."

"Okay, I'm off," Weenie said cheerily.

"See ya," Mort replied laconically, not looking up from his paper.

The screen door closed. A moment later it opened yet again and Weenie's head reemerged. "Mort, why don't you touch up the bench this morning? Repaint the place where Maggie sat."

"I'll try and get to it," Mort said. He looked up and added, "Hey, why don't you ask your buddy Jesus to perform a miracle and make the ass mark magically vanish?"

"Go to hell!" Weenie let the screen door slam. "Go to hell!" she barked again.

Mort winced. He turned back to the *Collier Current*, opened the sports page and was studying the Atlanta Braves baseball box scores when the screen door creaked open yet a third time. Weenie stormed out and marched toward her brother. He looked up as she stood over him, arms akimbo.

Mort cowered. "What?"

She glared. "Listen," she snarled, "I've really had it with you. Let's go ahead and have it out."

He leaned further away from her. "Have it out?"

32

"Mort, you know I take my faith seriously. I am a frail, fallible human, just like all of us. Just like you. I don't pretend to have all the answers in life, and I don't know exactly who or what God is. But I believe Jesus Christ is my Lord and Savior, and I pray every night that He is, and I am bloody well sick and tired of you making fun of Christianity and belittling my faith."

"Gosh, sis. I'm sorry if—"

Weenie wasn't finished. "Just stop it, okay? Not another word out of you!"

Mort watched her storm back to the house. The screen door slapped shut one last time. He looked up again at the sky. It was still a brilliant cobalt blue, but the day didn't seem so terrific anymore. He folded the newspaper and walked to the garage to get the can of white paint and a brush. The *Collier Current* would go under the bench to catch the drippings.

Chapter 7

I T WAS A LITTLE AFTER four in the morning. Mort was pouring freshly brewed coffee into his thermos when he heard a soft knock on the back door. Jimmy quietly stepped in and whispered, "Mornin', bro."

"Mornin'," Mort answered quietly over his shoulder. "Let me take care of my coffee; then I'm good to go."

Jimmy leaned against the old Formica counter top and whispered again, "I left the truck out on the road 'cause I didn't want to wake anybody." He pushed his billed cap back on his head, revealing a thick shock of blond hair with streaks of gray that curled around his ears. He was a stocky fellow, a man one would imagine had played lineman on his high school football team, which he had.

Mort screwed the thermos lid and grinned. "You coulda set off a cannon, and Maggie wouldn't hear it."

"What about Weenie?"

"Well, yeah, she would hear it."

Jimmy casually scanned the room, looking for nothing in particular. His gazed halted at the window over the sink. "You know these feeders are supposed to be on the outside of the glass, don't you?" he asked.

"I do," Mort said. "You put 'em on the outside if you want to feed a bird. Put 'em on the inside when you want to kill a bird."

"What?"

"It's very complicated," Mort whispered. "I'll explain it when we get in the truck."

Mort handed his thermos to Jimmy, grabbed his fishing rod and tackle box, and turned off the kitchen light. They walked down the oyster shell drive way under brilliant stars that sparkled in the deep cloudless night. Mort placed his gear in Jimmy's boat that rested secure on its trailer behind the truck.

Just east of town, Jimmy eased onto the four lane highway heading south and turned his radio to a country music station. Except for the pickup's low droning and the Gatlin Brothers' smooth crooning, all was quiet.

∽∾

Mort and Jimmy had met in fifth grade. During their friendship, now going on a half-century, there not many things they hadn't talked about. Still, heading south under a pre-dawn sky, they engaged in a few fragments that could almost pass for conversation.

"You hear what they're catchin' off Dauphin?" Mort asked.

"Nope. We'll find out soon enough."

Mort sipped his black coffee. Ten minutes, later he cocked his head toward the window and looked up. The stars twinkled and danced as though they were sentient beings.

"Nice night," Mort observed.

"Yep. Nice and bright."

Another long interlude. The mellifluous voice of Patsy Cline floated into the cab. *I go out walkin' after midnight. Out in the moonlight just like we used to do. I'm always walkin'....*

Jimmy turned the volume up. "God, she's the greatest," he sighed.

"Was," Mort said.

"What do you mean?"

"I mean *was*. She's dead."

"I know she's dead, you numbskull, but she's still great," Jimmy said.

"How can you be a great—present tense—singer when you're six feet under?"

Jimmy bit his lower lip. Patsy Cline had stopped walking after midnight. "You know," Jimmy snapped, "because of your stupid comments and my stupid decision to try and correct your stupid idea, we have now missed one of the great songs by one of the greatest singers who IS. Get it? IS."

Mort slurped his coffee, and then muttered, "Sorrree."

Silence in the cab. Jimmy shifted into fourth gear and said sharply, "Here's another dead singer. Do you mind if I listen to him?"

"Be my guest."

They drove on in an edgy silence, listening to Roy Orbison, but that edge would melt away as it had a hundred times before and the long friendship would get back on track. Mort reached toward Jimmy and offered his laden thermos lid. "Coffee?"

Jimmy reached for it. "Thanks." No edge.

❧❧

A soft pink glowed on the eastern horizon. The dark forms of the passing tree line gradually became more distinct. Mort offered more coffee, and Jimmy took more.

Patsy Cline came on the radio again. Jimmy looked over at Mort and said, "Okay. Here she is again, still dead and still great. Now shut your yap and let me listen in peace."

"Aye, aye, Cap'n," Mort said, saluting. "Yap shut, sir."

Jimmy turned the volume up. *Crazy. Crazy for thinking my love could hold you. I'm crazy for trying and crazy for crying....*

The sun was just peaking over the sand dunes as Jimmy backed his boat trailer down the ramp and watched, through his rear view mirror, as the old eighteen foot outboard slipped smoothly into the great salty waters of the Gulf of Mexico. Mort was standing on the shore holding the bow line to arrest the outward drift of the boat. He looked to his left at the rising sun and then southward out four miles at the southern most point in Alabama, Dauphin Island.

Jimmy eased forward, pulled the empty trailer up the ramp out of the water and parked over by a tree line.

&⯌&

A light westerly breeze rippled the surface of the Gulf. Mort, at the bow, held the boat against the dock. "You ready?" he called over his shoulder to Jimmy who was sitting on the stern bench seat.

"Hold just a sec," Jimmy said. "Let's think now. We got our tackle and bait?"

"Right."

"The cooler. Ice. Beer?"

"Right."

"Extra gas?"

"And right again, Cap'n," Mort said.

"Okay," Jimmy said. "Keep holding 'til I get her started."

Jimmy stood, faced aft and gripped the pull cord on his old twenty-five horsepower black Mercury outboard motor. One mighty pull. Chuga-chuga. No start. Another pull. No start. He opened the throttle on the engine's long handle and pulled the choke. He leaned in to the Mercury, this time gripping the pull cord with both hands. "Come on, you mutha," he grunted. He gave a mighty pull. Another weak chuga-chuga and a faint sputter. Then nothing.

"Goddammit!"

"Please, James," Mort whined, feigning offense. "Do not take the Lord's name in vain."

Jimmy wiped glistening sweat from his brow. "Well, if he would give me a little help with this fucking motor, I might speak a little nicer." With that he bent again over the recalcitrant Mercury, gripped the cord with both hands and gave an angry, hard yank. So hard that the boat rocked and swerved from the dock. Mort lost his hold on the dock and the boat drifted away. He reached out in vain. Jimmy was still facing aft, glaring down at his outboard, trying to decide on his next move. Mort stretched and reached again grabbing a fist full of humid Alabama air. "Shit!" he muttered.

Jimmy turned around and observed that they were underway. "What the hell did you do?"

"What did I do? What did you do? You pulled the boat away," Mort said.

"No, I didn't!"

"Yes, you did!"

The two grown men stood in the small boat facing one another in an infantile argument as their vessel slowly drifted away from shore. This, for anyone watching, seemed like an episode of *The Keystone Cops go to Sea*.

"Just sit down and be quiet," Jimmy said as he sat down himself.

All was quiet for a minute. A lone seagull glided overhead. Jimmy wiped his brow again. "Hand me my mallet," he said. "It's under your seat."

"The mallet?"

"Yes, asshole, the mallet."

"I don't under—"

"Mort, please just toss me the mallet. I am the skipper here, and I know what I'm doing."

Mort found the mallet and tossed it.

Jimmy missed the catch and the wooden hammer hit him in the nose. "Dammit!" He gently laid the mallet on the seat beside him. He stood and then quietly addressed his motor. "Okay, Quirky Merky, we've been through this before. This is your last chance before you know what."

He opened the throttle full and gave another maximum pull. No start. "That's it you little bastard," Jimmy snarled. He grabbed the mallet and wacked the outboard housing on the left and then the right side. The bad news was that he cracked the motor housing. The good news was that on the next pull old Quirky Merky sprung to life. Jimmy shot a triumphant fist in the air and exulted, "All those years of reading *Popular Mechanics* really pays off!"

As they headed out of the inlet, Jimmy increased speed and glanced at his watch. Seven-ten. He shouted over the drone of the engine, "I think it's time for a beer."

Mort reached for the cooler. "Past time, I should say." He shouted over the drone of the engine, "Salt water spray on our faces. Wind in our hair and beer in our throats. It doesn't get much better that this."

They fished for an hour, drifting along the western shore of Dauphin Island. It was still early morning, but between them they had already finished off a six pack. Beer and no fish tend to lead to conversation, even among men.

"So how's it goin' with you stayin' at Maggie's?" Jimmy asked.

Mort arched his rod and gave a lazy tug on his line, "Oh, I don't know. Not too bad, I guess." He scanned the island shoreline for a time. "Maggie's a weird duck. She can't hear a damned thing and can't remember anything. Anything except bad stuff about me, then her mind's like a steel trap."

"Why doesn't she like you?"

"Dunno." Mort reached for his beer. "She's always after me to do work around the house."

"Her house," Jimmy noted.

"Yeah. Her house,"

"Like what work?"

"Like repairing and painting her big garden bench."

"Like what else?"

"Oh, I don't know. Just stuff."

"Maggie's giving you free room and board, isn't she?"

"Room, yeah. We buy most of the food."

Jimmy reeled in and hooked on a fresh clam strip. He cast out far toward the shore. Watching his tackle plop into the water, he asked, "Why don't you get a job in town?"

Mort sighed. "Oh, I don't know. Just not sure really."

"You're right," his friend chided. "You don't want to rush into anything. You're not even sixty yet."

"Fuck you." Mort spit over the side.

The summer sun sparkled on the water. Two sailboats glided in the distance, their bright white sails billowing in a freshening breeze. Jimmy, looking from behind his dark glasses, regarded his old friend for a long time. Finally, he said, "Let's go try the other side."

40

"Why not?" Mort said flatly.

They reeled in. Jimmy turned his attention to Quirky Merky. He pumped the gas line and opened the throttle. Mort held up the mallet. "You need this?"

"Hope not." Jimmy gave the pull cord a yank, and the old outboard engine came to life.

They rounded the western tip of the island and turned eastward toward a long sandy spit of land. Dark clouds were gathering in the distance, far to the west along the Mississippi coastline. Jimmy turned the boat in a wide arc around the southern tip of the spit. Ahead, pelicans were gliding in their own wide arc. Jimmy and Mort both knew that where there were birds there was likely to be fish. Jimmy slowed the boat, and then killed the engine. "Okay," he said. "Let's see what we got here." He looked over at Mort as they both worked fresh bait onto their hooks. "I think we need a solemn vow now. No more beer 'til we catch a fish."

"That's kinda extreme, don't you think?"

"The captain has spoken. No fish, no beer. We gotta incentivize ourselves."

Their lines were back in the water. The tide was carrying them slowly toward the pelicans that now were joined by several noisy seagulls. Jimmy lowered his dark glasses for a closer inspection. "There's gotta be somethin' cookin' over there."

Mort expressed no anticipation. He looked longingly at the blue cooler at his feet. "It's almost lunch time, don't you think?"

"I'm going to hold off a bit," Jimmy said. "Go ahead and have your sandwich if you want."

"Might do that," Mort replied. "But with that thick bread and all, one's gotta have something to wash it down with."

"Nice try, buddy. Sandwich is okay. But no fish, no beer."

Mort spit over the side. "This is a stupid way to fish."

But stupid or not, fish that way they did. The sun was now high overhead and the air was turning sultry. Except for a lone pelican serenely bobbing with the gentle undulations of the Gulf, the birds had all disappeared. Mort wiped his brow. "This is bordering on no fun."

Jimmy, ever the optimist, clearly wanted to keep fishing. He tried to distract Mort from his funk. "What's Weenie up to these days?"

"Nothing much. Looks after the house. Keeps Maggie and me from killing each other."

"You know, I think you might want to—"

Mort stopped him. "Hey, I think I got something!" He pulled his rod back gently, waited, then started to slowly reel in. "It's a small one," he said, reeling in cautiously. "Still there."

Jimmy reached for the net and held it over the railing, watching the surface of the water. Mort saw the top end of his steel leader wire emerge. "Here she comes."

Jimmy lowered the net. Mort reeled even more slowly, then said, "Okay…now!"

Jimmy deftly scooped the net down and under the catch. The dripping round net emerged, holding a large, fighting-like-hell—crab. Both men grunted. Disentangling his hook and line from the frantic catch, Mort said with muted satisfaction, "Well, at least I qualify for a cold brewsky."

Jimmy's mouth dropped open. "What?"

"What yourself."

"I said fish. Fish for beer. That's a damned crab and a female at that."

"Oh for chrissake, Jimmy. You act like this is a floating concentration camp."

Jimmy sighed. "Oh, go ahead."

Mort tossed the crab overboard. He stowed his rod and fetched himself a sandwich and a cold beer.

"Well," said Jimmy with dejected resignation. "I'll take my lunch, too."

"With beer?"

"With beer."

Mort held up two sandwiches wrapped in aluminum foil. "You want salami and swiss with lettuce and tomato, or swiss and salami with tomato and lettuce?"

Jimmy feigned deep indecision. "Gosh, they both sound so delicious. Oh, just surprise me."

Mort tossed him one of the sandwiches and then a beer. He looked behind him as he popped his own beer. "Lookin' a little dark back there. Are we okay?"

Jimmy slid his dark glasses down on his nose and peered over the top rims. "Ah, it's just an isolated cell. I don't think it's going to amount to much."

Chapter 8

WHILE THE BOYS FISHED OFF the lee of Dauphin Island, Weenie—back at the old house—was thinking about that night. Peas, mixed in with white rice, was one of Mort's favorites, and she would prepare it for him to go along with the chicken roasting in the oven. She sat on the back step shaded by the tangle of Scuppernong vines overhead. A large bag of fresh picked pea pods lay next to her on the step. A yellow kitchen bowl, close by on her other side, held bright green peas.

Weenie sang, almost in a whisper, as she split a pod and spilled more peas into the bowl.

> *Swing low, sweet chariot,*
> *Comin' for to carry me home.*
> *Swing low, sweet chariot, comin' for to___*

"Hey, there, Miss Roweena. Good afternoon."

Jonah's wife, Eugenia, had walked quietly up the lawn from the river path.

Weenie looked up, putting one hand holding a pea pod, to her chest. "Oh, you startled me!"

"I'm sorry," Eugenia said as she approached the house. "I should've called out sooner."

"No bother," Weenie said smiling. "It's nice to see you."

"Nice to see you, too."

"I am so sorry to hear about your sister."

"Well," Eugenia said, "we are, too. Oh, I loved her so. But she's with the Lord now, I's sure, and we'll all be together again one day." Eugenia forced herself to brighten her broad, round face and push on. She held her arms out straight holding an offering. "Jonah and I thought y'all might like this. Peach pie, fresh made."

Weenie put her work aside and stood. "Oh, Genia, bless your heart. You are so sweet." She took the pie in both hands and said, "Let me take this into the kitchen. How about some ice tea?"

"That'd be right nice, ma'am. Thank you."

The two women sat together on the white bench with the bag of pods and the yellow bowl on the ground between them at their feet. Beads of water glistened on the two glasses of cold, sweet tea.

Eugenia took a long, slow drink. "Gracious, that tastes fine," she said, then licked her lips.

"It is refreshing," Weenie agreed. "It's close today and getting hot. We may get a storm later."

Eugenia squinted and studied the sky. "Maybe."

Weenie sipped more ice tea, then asked, "How's Colie? I haven't seen her in the longest time."

"Oh, she's alright, I suppose, but I don't really know, to tell you the truth. You know, her husband ran off last year. Real sudden like. Colie took it real hard. She's just not the same Colie, and we don't see her too much these days."

Colie, Jonah and Eugenia's daughter, was now maybe in her fifties. There was a story around town that most folks, at least most of the older folks, knew about how Colie got her name. Jonah and Eugenia were expecting their first child. They were excited and, for some unknown reason, had become convinced that a boy was enroute. They hadn't given much thought to a boy's name and absolutely no thought to one for a girl. When the baby arrived, they asked the doctor, so the lore went, an older white pediatrician, Doctor Mathis, what name he thought might be good. He suggested Colitis.

"Colitis?" Jonah and his wife had said together.

"Yes," the doctor said. "It's a very pretty name, don't you think? Like a beautiful Greek goddess."

So, Colitis it was. And a big joke, too, it was among the white folks. When Roy Lee heard about the cruel prank, he stormed over to Doctor Mathis' office and darned near took his head off. But by that time, the official State of Alabama birth certificate had been filled out, signed and stamped. Baby girl: Colitis June Tunny. Maggie and Randy Lee tried to get the parents to officially change the name, but they never did. They did, however, take their advice to call their daughter Colie and to encourage everyone else to do likewise.

"I am so sorry," Weenie said. "It's hard, isn't it, being a mother and having your daughter in a bad state?"

"Oh, you got that right, Miss Roweena."

They sat together in silence for a minute, after which Eugenia said, "Give me some of those pods down there and let me help you."

"Oh, no," Weenie protested.

"Oh, come on. We's just talking here. Might as well finish up that bag."

So Weenie slid over to the edge of the bench and placed the bag and the bowl between them. "That's awfully nice of you," she said.

Eugenie smiled, took a double handful of pods, plopped them on the lap of her faded print dress and went to work. She deftly snapped a pod, fingered the peas into Weenie's bowl and picked up the conversation. "Daughters can be a handful, you know."

"That is for sure," Weenie said.

"And how is yours?" Eugenia asked. "You know, you were gone so long up in Memphis, I only seen your Daphne a couple of times and that was a long time ago."

"It's Dabney." Weenie said, "Yes, long time ago."

"She was such a pretty thing," Eugenia said, snapping another pea pod. "I expect she's almost grown now."

"She's over thirty."

"Oh, my Lord Almighty! Where does the time fly?" Eugenia asked. "How's Dabney doin'?"

Weenie stopped her work and rested her hands in her lap. She sighed and answered, "Alright, I suppose." She sighed again and went on, "Maybe kind of like your Colie. Dabney somehow just can't seem to get it together. She's flighty....disorganized. Always losing things."

"Married?"

"No. She and a boyfriend lived together for almost two years. I liked him a lot and was hoping they'd get married, but it didn't work out."

"I'm sorry," Eugenia said.

Weenie shrugged and sighed yet a third time. "She's a happy girl, though. Almost too happy sometimes. She does weird things like—"

"Well, look who's here," Eugenia exclaimed, interrupting.

Seymour was sauntering up from the river toward the ladies. He made a beeline for Eugenia and nuzzled her legs.

"Hey, get away!" Eugenia shouted, giving the dog a whack. "You're soaking wet, you old hound."

Seymour then sidled up to Weenie, who stiff armed him. Accepting rejection stoically, he wandered the yard, poking, sniffing, and peeing.

Weenie's bowl of peas was almost full, when Rose rounded the corner of the garage and stepped into view. "Well, there you are," Rose said.

"Hey, there." Weenie said, as she stood and walked to her.

Eugenia, remaining seated, waved. "Hi, there, Miss Rose."

Rose Jamison, Aunt Maggie's mystery driver, said, "I've been knocking and knocking at the front door, but nobody answered."

"Nobody answered 'cause nobody's in the house," Weenie replied.

"Well, I hope Maggie's in the house," Rose said.

"She is, but you know she's deaf as a post."

Eugenia, by this time, had turned full toward the two ladies and was engrossed in the exchange.

"Is Maggie ready?" Rose asked. "We're taking a ride this afternoon."

Weenie's eyes opened wide. "A ride? Where are you going?"

"I am not at liberty to say. You'll have to ask Maggie," Rose answered rather officiously.

Weenie regarded Rose for a long moment, but said nothing. She then turned to Eugenia. "Genia, would you mind going up to Maggie's room and tell her Rose is here for her mystery ride?" Weenie turned back to Rose and guided her toward the garden bench. "Come sit with me for a minute," she said. "I'm just finishing up here with these—"

Weenie stared down at the yellow bowl in the middle of the bench which was now empty. She turned ever so slowly and looked down at Seymour who was licking his lips, resting contentedly on the grass. If a dog can have a guilty expression, that was the look all over Seymour's face. He raised his head and gazed at Weenie with his one eye, silently begging for a little understanding, maybe even a little forgiveness. It was not to be.

"Seymour!" Weenie screeched as the dog closed his eye and cowered, waiting for the blow. "All afternoon! All afternoon I worked to do something nice for someone else and you, you wretched, one-eyed, pea-stealing miserable excuse for a mutt!"

Weenie raised her arm, but before she could exact corporal punishment, the back screen door creaked open. Eugenia stepped out followed by Maggie who was looking a little disheveled and more than a little confused. "Who's here for me?" Maggie mumbled as she stepped onto the grass.

Weenie, still preoccupied with the canine pea thief, poured the remains of her ice tea on Seymour and swung the pod bag into the side of his cowering head. The poor dog yelped, whimpered, and scooted, tail between his legs, off toward the river. Weenie, totally exasperated, turned just in time to hear Rose call out as she rounded the garage with Maggie on her arm, "Be back later."

Chapter 9

MEANWHILE, DOWN ON THE GULF, Jimmy and Mort continued their lackadaisical pursuit of fish. They ate and drank in silence with Mort periodically glancing back over his shoulder. After a while Jimmy, speaking through a mouthful of sandwich, said, "So, we were talking about Weenie before."

"What?"

"Weenie."

"What about her?"

"We were talking about her a bit ago."

"Right," Mort said. He sipped his beer, then added, "You were kinda sweet on her in high school, weren't you?"

"Yeah, a little bit," Jimmy said.

"Ever date her?"

"Naw. Thought about it once or twice, but no." Jimmy recast and added, "Pretty amazing she could be so good lookin' and have such an ugly-ass brother. Are you sure you weren't adopted?"

"Fuck you, man," Mort snarled.

The breeze came again, cooler and more brisk than before, and buffeted the boat.

"So besides cleaning house and keeping you from murdering your aunt, what's she up to these days?"

"She spends a lot of time with her Bible thumpin' girlfriends."

"Why, Mortimer Boozer, I am surprised that you would make such a nasty, religiously biased utterance."

"Yeah, right."

"You've been that way forever," Jimmy said. "I even remember you in Sunday school. First Baptist was Worst Baptist or First Baddest or whatever."

"I know. My folks didn't think that was too funny."

"What a surprise," Jimmy chortled. "What's your big problem with the church anyway?"

"Aw, you know."

"Actually, I don't. I know you always make fun of the church, but what do you really think?"

"What do I really think?" Mort pondered the question. "Let's see." he started, "I think there might be a supreme being of some sort. Most folks think so. I think all religions may have a piece of the puzzle, but nobody's got it all. That's why I don't cotton to those people, especially those TV preachers, who think they know it all."

"How do you know they don't?" Jimmy asked.

"How do I know? I don't know. I just don't think they do, that's all."

Jimmy shifted his weight in the back of the boat. "Well, there's some rigorous logic for you."

Mort didn't say anything.

Jimmy pressed on. "What do you think of the Bible?"

"Well, that's another thing," Mort said, getting slightly animated. "It's about talking snakes and angels. People living in whales and dead folks coming up out of their graves and walking around town." Mort paused, and then added, "I'm just not sure."

"But you're sure enough to make fun of it all, and you're sure enough to piss off your sister over it."

Mort closed his eyes. "I'm not sure," he said. "Nobody can be sure about God and all that stuff. We're just these teeny weeny creatures on this teeny weeny planet in this teeny weeny solar system in this teeny weeny....."

"Okay!" Jimmy snapped. "I get it." He reeled in, checked his bait and cast again. He waited for his sinker to hit the Gulf floor then reeled in a couple of turns. "So," he said slowly, "what do you think of Jesus?"

"Ah yes, Jesus," Mort said. "You know I tried to have a calm conversation with my sister once about Jesus. But she became pretty uncalm pretty quick, so we never got very far."

"So if she had managed to stay calm, what would you have said?"

Mort grabbed his beer can, but upon shaking it, realized it was empty. He shrugged and said, "I would have shared with her that I admired Jesus greatly."

"Seriously?"

"Seriously. His teachings about how to live and how we should treat each other are right on. And he was brave. I mean really brave. To go through all what he did at the end there because of what he believed? Man, that's courage."

"So what's the problem?" Jimmy asked.

"The problem is he talked about some other stuff I just don't buy."

"Like?"

"Like—there's a devil. A real devil that he argued with up on the roof of some house. And like there's a hell and, if we don't believe in Jesus, then we're going there for all eternity."

"And?"

"And," Mort said, "that sounds like extortion to me."

Jimmy was stunned. "Extortion?"

"Yeah. Extortion. You either believe in me or you're going to hell. I call that a pure Mafia-style threat."

"Oh, come on, man. I don't think it's that way. But also, you know, if Jesus is really God, then you gotta take it all pretty seriously."

Another brisk wave of cool air from the west rippled the water.

"So you don't think Jesus was God?" Jimmy queried.

Mort sniffed. "Don't know for sure," he said, "but no, I don't think he was God, if there is such a thing."

At that moment, literally right out of the blue, as they say, came an ear-shattering, end-of-the-world explosion. Jimmy was thrown to the bottom of the boat where he landed on his back cracking the middle seat in half. Mort let his fishing pole fly in the air while he involuntarily arched backward falling overboard. It wasn't actually the end of the world. It only seemed like it. Totally sudden and unexpected. Just as suddenly, all was eerily quiet.

Jimmy painfully righted himself and sat dazed back by the engine, muttering, "Holy shit."

Mort, in the water up to his shoulders, was clinging to the boat. "What the hell was that?"

"Lightning," Jimmy said.

"Lightning?" Mort spat out some Gulf water. "Can't be. Sun's out."

"Not for long," Jimmy said. "Look up."

Mort clung to the side of the boat and followed his friend's gaze to the heavens just in time to see a blue-black wall of sky close around the sun and cover it. "Oh my god!" he wailed. "Give me a hand. Quick!"

Mort had managed to raise himself out of the water just enough for his arms, up to his arm pits, were over the railing and in the boat. He was frightened, moving rapidly toward panic. "Jimmy, help me! Quick!"

Jimmy, still dazed and aching, stood unsteadily in the rocking boat and stepped over the broken middle seat. He reached down and gripped Mort's outstretched arm. "Slowly now," he cautioned. But Mort was not in any mood to go slow. Pulling on Jimmy's arm, he got the upper half of his stomach to the rail, but in doing so, he pulled his erstwhile rescuer toward him.

Jimmy shouted, "Stop! You're gonna capsize us!"

With the weight of both men now on the port side, the boat heeled at a dangerous angle. It would have capsized but for Jimmy's violent jerk that broke their grip. His desperate maneuver allowed the boat to right itself, but simultaneously propelled Jimmy backward, launching him overboard on the starboard side. And now, for the second time that day, the boat was adrift without the benefit of human steerage.

Jimmy surfaced and reached for the rail on his side while his soaking Atlanta Braves baseball cap floated behind him. His hair matted down to his brow, his dark glasses rested in a cock-eyed fashion on his nose and over one eye. The two men, resembling two half drowned dogs with their four front paws clinging to the boat, regarded each other athwart ship.

54

The sky was rapidly darkening. It started to rain. Thunderous lightning struck again. Mort was wide-eyed. "Oh God, we're gonna die out here!"

Jimmy shouted, "Man, get a grip! Now take a deep breath. Here's what we're gonna do. You hold tight on your side and pull down while I get in over here. Then I'll slowly—and I mean slowly—pull you in. Got it?"

Mort nodded submissively with a terrified expression.

"Okay. That's our plan, and we gotta execute it just right," Jimmy said.

Lightning struck again. Mort flinched. "If we don't hurry we're going to GET executed."

Mort calmed down slightly and did what he was told while Jimmy, amidst considerable groaning and cursing, managed to grunt himself back into the boat. The rain was now a driving torrent.

"Okay, ready?" Mort asked.

"Wait a minute. Gotta catch my breath."

"Come on, dammit!" Mort shouted.

"Here." Jimmy tossed Mort the bitter end of the anchor line. "Tie this around you. Now you come up as best you can. I'm staying on this side, and I'll pull you."

Another violent crack from on high.

"Oh, Jesus," Mort whimpered.

"I think you might have really pissed Him off," Jimmy replied. "Let's talk about Him later."

Mort managed to claw himself up enough so that he was cantilevered, somewhat akin to a beached whale, over the port railing.

Jimmy pulled one last time, hauling his dead weight cargo into the bottom of the boat. He let Mort lie still gasping while he moved aft toward Quirky Merky. In spite of the wind, the thunder, and lightning, old (occasionally) reliable Quirky mercifully started right up. "Yes!" Jimmy exalted. He slammed the engine into forward and opened the throttle, realizing only then that, in the shrouded darkness, he had no idea where he was heading. "Oh, crap." He slowed the boat.

Mort shouted, "What are you doing?"

Jimmy ignored him. Instead, he carefully gauged the forward slant of the wind and rain and studied the water and the direction of the waves.

"Jimmy!"

"Shut up a minute."

Jimmy opened the throttle half way and turned to follow the general direction of the weather. He guessed that they and the storm were both heading eastward. He then turned to more port heading, he hoped, toward the south coast of the island. He increased speed. The waves were now off their port beam, and the boat yawed and surged as it churned through the downpour.

Mort turned aft again and stared at Jimmy. "You have life jackets, right?" he asked.

Jimmy shouted back, "Yes. I have four. They're back at the house."

Mort, now sitting upright, dropped his head to his chest and shot his hands, balled into fists, skyward with a plaintiff cry into the storm, "Save me, Lord! My captain is a blithering idiot!"

That captain, with rain flying in his face, shouted back, "Oh, ye of little faith. You are alive, you are in the boat, and the engine's running. What more could you ask for?"

Mort glared at Jimmy until another lightning bolt crackled nearby, sending him diving down onto the broken middle seat.

❧❧

The drenched fishermen motored on blindly, Jimmy silently hoping his dead reckoning instincts were good. Mort again turned back toward Jimmy. "You know where you're going?"

"Absolutely!" Jimmy lied.

As they rocked and rolled through the storm, the torrent eased to a heavy downpour then quickly to a medium rain. The wind eased, and their visibility increased. Then, as though they were driving through a curtain, they suddenly found themselves in bright sunshine under an azure blue sky. In less than five minutes, they had gone from pounding wind and rain in deep darkness to brilliant light in a sultry stillness. Both men were open-mouthed. Jimmy fumbled for his dark glasses. His blind navigational guesses turned out to be off, but not terribly so. The storm had pushed them farther south and west than he had guessed. In fact, they were almost beyond Dauphin Island and nearing the shipping channel into Mobile Bay.

Jimmy idled the engine. Both men surveyed their surroundings. The far western tip of the Florida panhandle was visible in the distance to the east. The storm-from-hell was now to their south and moving away from them. Jimmy let the boat chug along unattended as he pulled his wet shirt over his head. Mort watched him and followed suit.

"We got any water in that cooler?" Jimmy asked.

Mort opened the cooler, searched through the slushy mix of water and ice and retrieved two bottles. He tossed one to his skipper and threw his head back and drank heavily from the second. He closed his eyes, basking in the warmth of the sun.

All was serene until Jimmy spoke. "So, bro, why don't we fish some more?"

Mort swallowed hard. "What? Are you nuts?"

Jimmy said, a bit sheepishly, "I just thought as long as we were out here—"

"Well, for starters," Mort barked, "in case you hadn't noticed, my fishing pole is no longer with us. Secondly, we damned near died back there. I haven't quite figured out what just happened. I'm exhausted. My arm hurts. And you want to fish?"

"Well, what do you want to do?" Jimmy asked.

"I want to get off the water. I want to get out of this friggin' boat, and I want to go home!"

"Okay, "Jimmy said. "You go home now, and Maggie's just gonna give you a bunch of work."

"I'll take my chances with her."

Jimmy sighed. "It's a beautiful day now, but alright."

He gave Quirky Merky more gas, turned slowly to port, and started the long run around the eastern end of the island.

The sun was starting its descent in the west as they eased into the dock on the mainland. Jimmy killed the engine and said, "Hold her there while I get the—" He felt his pockets with both hands. "Shit."

"What?" Mort asked.

"My keys."

"Oh, god," Mort whined pitifully.

Jimmy, already bending low to unlatch his tackle box, called forward to Mort, "Look in that bow compartment."

"Jimmy, how would they get in there?"

"Just look, will you!"

Mort, too weary to argue further, dutifully sat down on the small bow seat and opened the little door to the compartment. The truck keys, of course, were not inside. While Mort still had his head down, almost in the compartment, and was starting to verify that the keys were not there, the boat, of course, began to drift away from the dock. Jimmy meanwhile finished his own futile search of his tackle box and looked up, realizing that they were once again underway.

"Mort, goddammit! Look what you've done!"

Mort looked up and simply closed his eyes. Fortunately, this time there was no need for further cursing or hammering. The outboard started on the first pull and the crisis was averted.

"Mort, please, please get the bowline now and tie it to the cleat on the dock."

Mort did as he was told, and said, "By the way, your fucking keys are not in the compartment."

"Thank you for that report," Jimmy muttered as he rummaged around the boat.

"Look in the cooler," he barked.

"They're not in the cooler!"

"Look in the cooler!"

The keys were not in the cooler. Jimmy sat, resting his arm on the engine. "Shit."

"Maybe they fell out of your pocket when you were helping me get back in the boat."

"Maybe." Jimmy said, "I doubt it." He reached for his shirt which was now dry. He wiped his perspiring face with the shirt then pulled it on over his head. "Stay here," he said. "I'll be right back."

A dirt road paralleled the shoreline and, from previous outings, the men knew there was a small tackle shop a half a mile around the bend.

Mort watched Jimmy disappear behind the sand dune at the bend, then opened the cooler for one last brew.

A half an hour later, as Jimmy rounded the bend on foot, he saw his truck parked down the launch ramp with the trailer partially in the water. Mort was sitting on the dock, facing away from him, watching a glorious sun set. Jimmy took no notice of the celestial spectacle. "Hey!" he called. Mort turned and gave him a laconic look. "How'd you get her started?" Jimmy asked.

"You know," Mort dead-panned as Jimmy approached him, "lucky thing that I, too, read all those *Popular Mechanics*. It was a pretty involved process. I went over to the truck and analyzed the situation carefully. Then I got in the cab, and I slowly turned key that was in the ignition all the time and, by golly, it just started right up."

Jimmy turned his gaze from Mort, looked over at the pick-up, and wiped his brow. "Well, I'll be damned," he said softly.

☙❧

It was twilight by the time they were on the road heading back to Collier Bluff. Jimmy extended his left hand out the side window and waved at an AAA tow truck as it passed them heading south.

Mort asked, "You know that guy?"

"Not personally. I'm sure he's responding to the call I made back at the tackle shop."

"Why didn't you call back after we—I—found your keys?"

"Guess I kinda forgot," Jimmy said.

"You're really a swell guy, you know," Mort observed dryly.

"Aw, he'll figure it out," Jimmy said, turning on the radio. Johnny Cash was rolling through Folsom Prison Blues. "Mort, we can talk about anything you want, but please don't get after any of these singers just 'cause they're dead."

Mort kept quiet for a few minutes, then said, "It was a helluva day, wasn't it?"

"Yep." Jimmy said, "Won't forget this one for a while." Then, trying to sound real serious, he added, "You know, what you said out there about poor ol' Jesus almost got us killed."

"Hey," Mort said, "I said some very nice things about Him."

"I don't know, man. I think you might've really pissed Him off."

"Oh, bullshit. Don't give me that. I know you never go to church unless Jane Ellen makes you."

Jimmy said, "Well, I go often enough to keep my options open. But you're going to Hell, man." Then he chuckled.

Mort looked out his side window at the gathering night, watching the sky fade to black. "It's not funny, Jimmy." He leaned back in his seat and closed his eyes.

"Well, I gotta tell you," Jimmy said, "I think God can be pretty funny sometimes. He's got a real sense of humor." Jimmy turned the radio down. "You know, I had an uncle, Uncle Steeney. One of my mom's brothers. He was kinda like you, only a lot smarter. But kinda like you."

No reaction from the passenger seat.

Jimmy continued, "He was always reading. All kinds of books. Went to church once in a while, but not too much. He kept a diary and, when he died, my mom gave it to me. Really interesting stuff. You should read it."

Mort, his eyes still closed, did not respond.

Jimmy looked over at him. "You awake?"

"Yes, I'm awake."

"Okay. Maybe I'll bring the diary over to you sometime."

Mort yawned. "Sure. You do that."

Chapter 10

THE SPRAWLING YARD BEHIND MAGGIE's house sloped down to the river, the gentle Monacoosa River that flowed south through the center of Collier Bluff. In the late afternoon, one could sit in the garden behind the house and watch the setting sun throw sparkling diamonds on the river. And sometimes at night, when the moon was full, little pieces of sunlight would bounce off the moon and dance their shimmering dance upon the water. The steady, silent flow of the Monacoosa was the great constant in the march of the Boozer generations and indeed all inhabitants, black and white, of Collier Bluff and McCann County, Alabama.

Every few years, a hurricane or tropical storm would roar up from the Gulf of Mexico, swelling the river and causing it to breach her muddy banks. Folks around town said the Monacoosa flooded once in a while just to make sure people didn't forget their riparian neighbor.

It was early morning. A few rays of sun slanted through magnolia leaves and landed out on the marsh grass beyond the river. Mort had poured himself a second mug of coffee and stepped down off the back steps. He was heading toward the white garden bench when he heard a rhythmic swishing sound out by the water. He looked up to see Jonah bent over, arcing and swooping a metal knifed scythe. A whoosh and a thrash. A whoosh and a thrash. Mort startled him as he came up behind. "Mornin', Jonah."

He turned. "Oh, you scared me. Mornin' to you, Mister Mort."

"What are you doin' there?" Mort asked.

"Miss Maggie asked me to cut back these bushes so she could see the river better."

"You know, she won't remember she told you," Mort said

"I knows that, Mister Mort," Jonah said, "but I remember, and she pays me to do what she asks me to do. I want to get it done 'fore it gets too hot."

Jonah probably did want to finish early, but he apparently wasn't too upset at a chance for a break. He pulled his old red and black handkerchief from his back pocket, wiped his face and neck, and sat down on a log. Mort joined him, putting his elbows on his knees and cupping his mug with both hands.

The morning was warming up fast. Jonah slapped at a horse fly. "Heard you had a real time fishing in the Gulf last week."

"You could say that," Mort said.

"Catch anything?"

"Oh, yeah," Mort said brightly. "About fifteen. All big ones."

Jonah arched his eye brows. His white teeth gleamed. "Mister Mort, a man might be going to Hell lyin' like that."

Mort laughed. "Naw, actually we got skunked." Mort drank his coffee and looked out at the river. "But since you brought up Hell," he said, "let me ask you a question."

Jonah pushed his straw hat back on his head. "Don't make it too hard." he said, "I'm not real good with hard questions."

"I won't," Mort said. He hesitated, then sallied forth. "Do you believe in Jesus?"

"Oh, that's not a hard one, Mister Mort. Yes sir, I do!"

A large blue heron, wings set, glided low above the water. Shortly after Mort and Weenie moved in with their aunt, they began seeing a large blue heron out by the river. They assumed it was always the same bird, and they named their blue feathered friend Aaron. Certainly this was Aaron that now circled just upstream, glided southward and landed on the far bank of the river.

"So, Jonah, okay, you believe in Jesus. But why?" Mort asked.

"Well, now that is a harder one," Jonah pushed his straw hat farther back on his head. "I've just gone to church all my life. All my relations have. Can't remember not going. So...well... I don't know really. I just think Jesus loves us all and wants to take care of us. That's what the Bible says."

"What about Hell?"

"What about it?"

"Well," Mort said, "let's say someone thinks Jesus' teachings are pretty good, but that he, this person, doesn't buy the idea that Jesus is really God. Would that person go to Hell?"

"Your questions are getting harder, Mister Mort," Jonah said. He looked skyward and pondered the question. Finally, he answered, "Well, that's kind of what the preachers say, especially the fire and brimstone ones. But I think maybe they're just trying to scare us into not sinning so much."

Mort threw his head back and drained the last of his coffee. They both studied Aaron strutting on stick legs along the far shore. Mort wondered if the bird ever wondered about Jesus. Maybe it will go to heron hell. He turned toward Jonah. "Do you think Jesus is pretty accurate with lightning strikes?"

"What?"

"I said do you think—"

At that moment, the kitchen screen door opened and slapped shut. Mort and Jonah turned toward the house. There she was, standing barefoot in her night gown, looking out at them through her bottle bottom glasses. "Jonah!" she graveled. "I'm not paying you to sit out there on that log."

"No, ma'am, I know," Jonah answered.

Maggie shouted again. "Who's that man there you're talking to?" She went on before Jonah could reply. "You tell him to skedaddle and not be bothering you."

"Yes, ma'am."

Maggie went back inside, the screen door slapping behind her. Jonah went back to work.

Mort headed to the house. He picked a grape from the vine, popped it into his mouth, and opened the door. In the kitchen, he refilled his mug and pushed open the swinging kitchen door to the dining room where he found his sister and Maggie having breakfast.

"Mornin,'" he said.

"Mornin', Brother," Weenie said.

Maggie looked up at Mort. "Good morning," she said flatly. "Haven't seen you in a while."

Chapter 11

A FEW WEEKS LATER, THIS TIME with a faint hint of fall in the air, a delightful, almost cool breeze off the river shimmered through the live oak trees and rattled the dry leaves of the magnolia tree. Mort and Weenie were in the kitchen getting ready to enjoy the sparkling morning in the garden. Weenie toasted English muffins and set Mort's Roll Tide mug and a second one for her on the counter. Mort reached for his Plexiglas bird feeder suctioned to the inside of the window. He disposed of the stale feed and refilled the tray with fresh seeds. Weenie, a bit stunned, but not totally surprised, watched the strange procedure. "Fresh seed," she observed matter of factly. "Boy, that'll fool ol' Karl for sure."

"You just wait," Mort said, putting the bag of bird feed back in the pantry.

They sat together in the garden, mugs in hand and a plate of warm muffins resting on the bench between them. Weenie looked suspiciously over at the vine by the back door. She opened her mouth to scold, but halted, deciding apparently she had insufficient evidence for an indictment.

"Maggie still sleeping?" Mort asked.

"I expect so." Weenie looked to the sky. "What a morning. I think this is my favorite time of year."

"It's nice alright," Mort said, adding, "What are you going to do today?"

"It's Wednesday," Weenie answered. "What do I do every Wednesday morning?"

"Oh, yeah. Forgot what day it was."

"And what are you doing today?" she asked.

"Oh," Mort sighed. His mind seemed to drift off somewhere. If he had a plan for the day, it was apparently not on the tip of his tongue. He sniffed, then coughed, then, in a kind of awkward way, he asked, "What would you think if I went with you to Bible study?"

Weenie held her mug still, poised a few inches from her lips. She turned ever so slightly and looked warily at him. "What?"

Mort stared out at the Monacoosa, watching a couple paddling their canoe against the current.

Weenie asked. "What's going on with you?"

Mort didn't respond.

"You really want to go?"

"I just thought it might be interesting."

"It's all women, you know."

"All the better."

Weenie continued to study his face, her own visage dark and suspicious. She said, "Mort, if you go there and make fun of the Bible or me, I swear I will strangle you with bare hands."

Mort laughed.

"I mean it, bro."

"I thought the Bible says it's a sin to murder," Mort said.

"In the case of a severely mentally ill person, such as yourself, it would be euthanasia. Definitely not a sin."

❧❧❧

So later that morning, Weenie and Mort climbed the porch steps of Miss Mavis's grand antebellum home on LaGarde Street. As they entered the large, high ceiling living room, Weenie said in a loud voice, "Good morning, ladies."

The good Christian women of Collier Bluff, most with coffee or coffee cake or unfinished sentences in their mouths, turned to the new arrivals.

"Ladies," Weenie said brightly, trying to mask her anxiety. "Good to see you all this morning. I brought a guest with me. Hope no one minds. Most of you know my brother—my much older brother—Mort."

Mort waved shyly. The group murmured their hellos and welcomes along with a couple of "I declares."

Weenie added, "Mort expressed an interest in the Bible and asked, if it was alright, could he join us today. I said Jesus welcomes all."

"Why He certainly does," Miss Mavis, the longtime leader of the group, agreed. "We are glad to have you with us, Mortimer."

The ladies milled around for another minute, refilled their cups, selected a final munchie and began to choose their seats. Mort followed suit, getting himself coffee and a large Danish pastry and headed for a chair in the back of the room. Miss Mavis, speaking in her Southern drawl, thick even for South Alabama, quieted the group and began the meeting by announcing, "In addition to Mister Boozer, we have a second visitor with us this morning. I would like you all to greet Linda Steele's great friend, Lila Gibney, who is visiting here from Atlanta." Mort, along with the rest, looked at the lady from Georgia.

Miss Mavis then prayed for the group, the town, the nation, and "all God's children". Mort kept his head bowed as long as he could manage before raising his head slightly to take another look at the lady from Atlanta. Her hair was a soft blond mixed with grey. Her summer tan contrasted beautifully against her pearl necklace, white blouse and navy blue skirt. Mort thought she was attractive. Very attractive, actually.

Miss Mavis brought her holy beseechings to a close and all heads, except Mort's which was already up, rose in unison. The attractive Mrs. Gibney opened her eyes and looked over at Mort who was mesmerized looking at her. She smiled slightly, then quickly looked down and opened her Bible. "Now ladies," their leader began, then correcting herself, "Ladies and, of course, Mister Boozer, who is with us—" When Mavis mentioned Mort's last name, the Gibney woman looked again at Mort with a strange puzzled expression.

Miss Mavis continued to hold forth. "—and it is with the wonderful grace of God that we are here together this morning to pray, to share, and to learn together the meaning of God's word." She rested her hands, palms up, on her knees. She closed her eyes and remained statue-like still for almost a minute. The room was still. Mort, even with an unchewed mouth full of pastry and his coffee up on his knee, felt compelled to freeze in place. Finally, the leader opened her eyes and took her Bible in both hands. "Now, let's all turn to the Gospel of Mark."

She raised her reading glasses that hung from her neck on a silver chain, marked the passage she wanted, and then lowered her glasses again. "This morning," she said, "we are going to explore a side of Jesus that not many people, I think, pay enough attention to. Or maybe just don't want to focus on. Jesus was a babe in the manger and a gentle savior whose love for us knows no bounds. But there is another side. Here we learn about Him and the money changers in the temple, and we see his wrath and his righteous anger. As a loyal daughter of the South, I kind of hate to invoke the words of that Yankee war song; but in fact, our actions sometimes give God no choice but to bring forth, as the song says, 'His terrible swift sword.'"

She looked down and read a few lines of Mark's Gospel, then looked up at the group and asked rhetorically, "Jesus, kind and loving?" She continued, "Of course, but his wrath can come sometimes like a lightning bolt from the sky."

This produced a gasp from the back of the room. Mort choked on his Danish and spilled his coffee.

Mavis craned her neck and zeroed in on him. "Mortimer, are you alright?"

"Yes, ma'am," Mort croaked, "just a little choked up back here." He looked up to see Weenie giving him a cold stare.

Miss Mavis set her glasses on the tip of her nose and looked down to her Bible. "Well, let's see. Where was I?"

One of the ladies said, helpfully, "You were at swords and lightning strikes."

"Oh, yes. Thank you."

After a rambling hour long discussion about Jesus' mean side, the Wednesday morning session of the Collier Bluff Bible Study—some around town referred to it as Collier Bluff BS—was brought to a close. All rose, with the ladies immediately launching into conversation and competing to see who could be the most helpful cleaning up. Meanwhile, Mort was on his hands and knees, sopping his spilt coffee with his paper napkin. He heard a lady's voice above him. "Can I help you?"

Mort raised his head slightly, seeing first two high heeled shoes, then a pair of nicely shaped legs, then the hem of a navy blue skirt. The Gibney woman was bending over him, offering her paper napkin.

Mort accepted it sheepishly, but gratefully, completed his clean-up, then stood. "Thank you very much," he said. "I appreciate it."

"Not at all," the lady said, smiling broadly. She looked directly at Mort and held his gaze for a moment. Then she said, "You don't know who I am, do you?"

Mort held his empty coffee cup in one hand and two wet paper napkins in the other. He stammered a barely decipherable apology.

The lady, obviously enjoying Mort's discomfort, said playfully, "I'll give you a hint." She said slowly, "Call—your—bluff."

Mort was still bewildered. Then, slowly his mouth opened and his eyes widened. "Oh, Lord," he sputtered, "you're Lila Ann?"

She burst a wonderful laugh. "Yes, sireee. I am Lila Ann," she gushed in a lilting Southern accent. She then put her arms around him, smothering Mort in a long, warm hug.

They disentangled. He stood back and looked at her. "You've really grown," he said, sheepishly adding, "That's probably the stupidest thing I've ever said."

A voice behind him observed, "I'm not sure that's even in your top one hundred stupid statements."

It was Weenie, of course. Mort introduced the two ladies. Weenie immediately asked her brother, "And how do you know each other?"

Mort grinned. "It's a long story. I'll tell you later."

Weenie got a ride home with a friend. Lila Ann's host reluctantly left her house guest in the uncertain care of Mortimer Boozer who had offered his long lost love a ride. Mort turned on to Gadsden Avenue and, per Lila's direction, parked in front of a large white clapboard house. They remained in the car and talked for an hour. Correspondence via the U.S. mail was their first topic of conversation.

"I wrote you," Mort complained, "but you never wrote back."

"I certainly did," Lila Ann said indignantly, "You never wrote *me* back."

"Well, I never got your letter."

"Well I wrote it."

"Did you mail it?"

"Yes, I mailed it. And I didn't use that juvenile call-your-bluff stuff." She proceeded to spell out Collier Bluff. She looked out the side window of the car for a moment, and then added, "You could have called me."

Mort did not respond. He glanced over at the pretty lady sitting next to him. "Can you believe that was almost fifty years ago?"

It was almost noon and the rising heat of the day prompted them to roll down their front windows. And on they talked. It got hotter, so Mort rolled the windows back up, started the engine and turned the air conditioner on full. Their conversation continued. He learned that Lila had married while she was still in college, had two boys, now grown men, in their thirties. Her husband had died two years ago. Lila learned from Mort that he was *taking some time off from his to career* to attend to his dear elderly and ailing aunt. He declined to discuss the nature of his *career* nor did he mention that his sabbatical had been going on for almost three years.

"Married?" she asked.

"No." Mort replied, "Just never found the right girl, I guess."

"Oh my," Lila Ann sighed.

Mort decided to revise and extend his remarks. "Ever since that cute girl from Atlanta never wrote me back, I've just been dying slowly of a broken heart."

She blushed. "Oh, go on," she said, pushing his shoulder.

They exchanged phone numbers and addresses and promised, really promised, to stay in touch.

Chapter 12

MORT PULLED HIS OLD PONTIAC into the driveway in front of Maggie's house and entered through the front door. Weenie was watering Maggie's potted plants in the hall.

"You were gone a long time," she said.

"Yes, well, we had a long talk. I dropped her off at her friend's house."

"Old girl friend?"

"Sort of."

Mort told her the whole story, even the part about the letter and the Call Your Bluff return address and him secretly pining away for her reply. "What are the chances," Mort said, "that the one time in my life I go to a Bible study class, I meet a girl from Georgia I was smitten with when I was a boy?"

"Oh, ye of little faith," Weenie teased. "God works in mysterious ways."

"Don't get started on me now," Mort said.

Weenie bent to give a large geranium a drink. "You gonna see her again?"

"Hope so," Mort said. He yawned. "I think I'll take a nap. Kinda tired. My PTSD must be kickin' in."

"Your PTSD?"

"Hey," Mort said, defensively, "you know I spent a year in Vietnam. Combat zone."

"Oh, come off it." Weenie said, "You were a corporal in the Army supply corps. Closest you ever came to combat was when that beer truck you were driving was two hours late and your own troops were so pissed they shot your tires out."

Mort squirmed. "I know. But it was very traumatic, and now it's post. Post traumatic. Anyway, I need a nap." Mort glanced at Weenie. "Besides, what do you know about trauma?"

Weenie turned with anger in her eyes. "I know more about it than you think, buster!" she snarled. "I was living up there in Memphis all those years with that sorry excuse for a husband. He was violent. It was scary. Yes, sir, I've had some trauma, you bet I have."

Mort started to say something, but Weenie wasn't finished. "At the same time I was trying to deal with that jerk, I had two miscarriages. You didn't know that, did you? And by the way, after the first one, I called you because I really needed to talk with someone and you never called me back."

"Gosh, Hon, I had no idea—"

Weenie still wasn't finished. "We couldn't have children. That's why we adopted Dabney. So then I have more trauma dealing with a tiny baby, who had her own traumatic beginning to life, and that sorry excuse for a husband. So I really don't need a lecture from you about how driving a beer truck in Vietnam was so terrible."

Weenie had said her piece and marched back to the kitchen. Mort followed her. She wiped her hands on a dish cloth, turned and pushed open the swinging door to the dining room. Unfortunately, Maggie was on the other side trying to decide whether she wanted to go into the kitchen. The first thump was the swinging door hitting Maggie. The second, Maggie's rump hitting the dining room floor, was followed by her cry. "Ouch! What in tarnation do you think you're doin' in there? Oh my Gawd!" she wailed.

Weenie rushed in to her aunt and bent over her. "Oh, Maggie, I am so sorry."

Mort stepped into the dining room. "Now, there is some real trauma! That's what I'm talking about."

"Shut up, Mort!" Weenie said, "Help me get her up."

Together they carefully lifted Maggie off the floor and into a chair. Mort retrieved her glasses from under the dining room table.

"Get her some water," Weenie commanded over her shoulder. "Are you hurt?" she asked Maggie. "Does anything hurt?"

"Yes, dammit!" Maggie croaked. "My whole body hurts. But I ain't dead yet."

Mort held a glass of water to her. "Here you go."

Maggie swatted it away, saying, "Get me some bourbon. Plenty of ice."

The seemingly indestructible Magnolia Boozer Paxton, it turned out, was only bruised and shaken. The only serious casualty was the already low regard she held for poor Mort. Despite Weenie's repeated attempts to explain what really happened, Maggie was convinced that Mort not only pushed the kitchen door into her, but did so on purpose.

∽∾

Peace, however, returned in the old home the next morning, thanks to Maggie's failing memory. At breakfast, Mort tried valiantly to strike up a conversation with his aunt. "How are you today, Aunt Maggie?" he inquired cheerfully.

She lifted her coffee cup and saucer to her lips and slurped. "Not too bad, I guess," she said, "except my ass is pretty sore."

"Oh my," Mort said, "I'm sorry to hear that."

"Me too," Maggie said. "Must have sat on the can too long this morning."

After a hearty breakfast of two cups of black coffee, Maggie shuffled herself upstairs to start her day. Weenie left for the grocery store. Mort repaired to the white bench in the garden with his *Collier Caller*. Pen in hand, he methodically read through the Help Wanted ads. He was distracted by the sound of oyster shells crunching out front.

"Top o' the morning, mate," Jimmy said as he rounded the back of the garage on foot.

Mort quickly put his pen away and turned to the sports page. "Well, what an almost pleasant surprise," he said.

Jimmy settled himself on the bench.

"Have a seat," Mort said after the fact.

Jimmy didn't get the dig. "Hey, I brought you something." He handed Mort a small dog-eared brown notebook. "You remember when we were fishing and I told you about my uncle and about him writing?"

Mort nodded.

"Well, here's his notebook. There's some interesting stuff in there."

Mort put the newspaper aside and opened the notebook. He slowly thumbed through it. He saw that most entries were only a paragraph or two. All were dated. The entry on the first page was January 1, 1938. The last, October 12, 1956.

"Looks like a diary," Mort said.

"Kind of," Jimmy said, "except it's not about him. It's all about him trying to figure things out."

Mort closed the notebook and laid it on the bench.

"Keep it for a while," Jimmy said, "but I want it back."

"Sure."

Jimmy squinted up into the sky. "It's gettin' hot."

"Very astute observation," Mort replied.

"So hot now that a cold beer would really hit the spot."

"Ah, an observation with a motive."

Mort went into the house and returned with two cold ones. Two cans flip topped open and whooshed simultaneously. Mort took in his first swallow as he reached with his free hand for Uncle Steeney's book. He read a random entry:

December 4, 1941--- Here I go again. These nights, these December nights are the worst. Days shorter, nights longer, colder, darker, depressing as hell. I think all of us are driven by fear. Fear of attack, fear of hunger, fear of loss, fear of embarrassment. Most of all, fear of dying. Going stone cold dead for all eternity. Feel that way now. I wonder again, oh grace, yes again about the Big Guy. Did he create us or the other way around?

Stopping for tonight.

No. Not yet. Just now something coming over me. I sense danger. Foolish? Something bad, maybe real bad, is looming. Steeney out.

Jimmy smacked his lips. "Nothin' better than a cold beer in the morning."

Mort, still flipping through the notebook, was silent.

Then Jimmy said, "Listen, my man, I've got a problem, thanks to you."

Mort closed the notebook and looked up. "A problem? Thanks to me?"

"Jane Ellen said you went to the Ladies' BS Wednesday. What's that all about?"

"Just curious," Mort said.

"Just curious, huh?"

"Yeah, what's your problem?" Mort asked.

"My problem, for your information, is that my old lady is now giving me a ration. Says I don't have the cojones to go there."

"I expect she's right about that." Mort said.

"Oh, bull shit," Jimmy said, crunching his empty can over his knee.

"Well, why don't you prove her wrong?"

Jimmy jutted his jaw and contemplated the challenge. "Okay, cojones man, I'll pick you up next Wednesday. Nine forty-five. I need a witness."

"Believe me, Jimmy, you're gonna have plenty of witnesses and they'll blab about you all over town."

Chapter 13

WEDNESDAY'S SKY WAS A GLOOMY, rainy gray, but most folks around were buoyed by the cooler air and the respite from a fall drought.

Weenie had left early for Bible study so, she claimed, she could help with the coffee cake. In fact, her head start was to give the Christian ladies of Collier Bluff due warning that this day not one, but two, men would be joining them.

Mort swayed on the front porch swing waiting for Jimmy, absently watching the rain cascading off the roof. Seymour snoozed behind him. At the sound of crunching oyster shells, he stood to walk down to Jimmy's truck. But it was not Jimmy who had arrived. Instead, it was a light blue, two-door sedan that came into view and stopped in front of the house. The driver got out and hustled through the rain up to the porch. Seymour lifted his head ever so slightly to look at the stranger. The old hound almost, but not quite, mustered the energy to stand up and examine the man more closely. Instead, he laid his head back on the wooden floor and closed his one eye.

The visitor wiped his fingers on his khaki pants and extended his hand in greeting. "Good morning, sir," he said with an upbeat air. "My name is Charles Lodger with Face To Face Custom Windows out of Mobile."

Mort stood and grasped Mister Lodger's hand. "Yes sir, "Mort said. "You were here a few weeks ago telling us about your windows."

"I was?" Lodger said.

"You were indeed and we, my sister and I, told you then that we weren't in the market for new windows."

"You did?"

"Yes."

"Well, I am so sorry to have bothered you this morning. My apologies."

"That's alright," Mort said kindly, after which Mister Lodger descended the porch steps and departed the premises.

Jimmy arrived five minutes later. Mort trotted hunched over out to the truck and jumped in on the passenger side. "Let's roll," he said. But Jimmy just let the truck idle in neutral. "Come on, man," Mort said.

Jimmy turned to Mort. "Are you sure we want to do this?"

Mort said, "Well, what have we here? A big ol' Alabama red neck with a honking bull of a truck afraid to join some little ol' ladies who are hungering for God's word?"

Jimmy stared through his swishing windshield wipers, grunted, and slowly put the truck in gear. As he pulled out of Maggie's driveway, Mort asked, "Got your Bible?"

"What?"

"You can't go in there without your Bible."

What!" Jimmy pulled off the road. "Are you serious?"

Mort guffawed. "Relax, man. This is not going to kill you."

❦❦

Jimmy followed behind Mort up the wide veranda stairs into the large foyer and finally into the Miss Mavis's living room. The ladies hushed as they stepped into the room. Miss Mavis gave them a wide, warm smile. "Welcome gentlemen," she greeted.

A lady in the group observed loudly, "Looks like integration has really come to Alabama!"

Mort, the Bible study veteran, maneuvered to the back of the room and took a seat against the wall. Jimmy followed him, but was cut off by a lady who was making a beeline for the one available seat next to Mort. She sat and said brightly, "Morning, Mort." It was Lila Ann.

Jimmy, looking like the loser in a game of musical chairs, was relegated to a sofa in the front of the room.

Miss Mavis dinged her little silver bell. "A great good morning to all of you." she said. "And, Mortimer, welcome back, and you have brought another visitor. Would you care to introduce him?"

"Yes, ma'am," Mort answered from the back of the room. "I think a lot of you know Jimmy Claggett. He's the one up front there. The one who's not a woman."

Miss Mavis had to ding-ding her bell again to quiet the group. Order was restored and Mavis led an expansive prayer for the Christian women of Collier Bluff, the State of Alabama and all their brothers and sisters throughout the South. She presumably thought those living north of the Mason-Dixon Line were either already safe in God's hands or, more likely, beyond redemption. She donned her tethered spectacles and pushed her Bible out onto her knees to get her line of sight beyond her large obstructing bosom. She cleared her throat and began. "Today, I thought we would consider the mystery of God's work. It is often hard, is it not, to know God's plan and God's ways. We are such lowly creatures, like ants on a watermelon trying to figure out where they are and what they are dealing with."

Jimmy looked over at Mort with an expression that seemed to say "huh?" Mort, preoccupied with something to do with the lady next to him, missed the gaze.

Miss Mavis plunged further into God's mystery. "As Paul writes in his letter to the Corinthians, 'For now we see through a glass darkly, but then face to face.' So let's take some time this morning to try and understand what it is that we cannot understand about God's will before we come face to face with Him."

Meanwhile, in the back of the room, Lila Ann's bare knee had shifted ever so slightly as to be against Mort's knee. Needless to say, Mort's thoughts were drifting far away from God's mystery.

The meeting ended precisely at the top of the hour. The ladies stood and began to talk, move chairs around and carry napkins, food and cups into the kitchen. Jimmy, standing awkwardly alone, spotted Mort and hurried toward him. Mort was holding Lila Ann's two hands in his two hands and clearly enjoying their conversation.

Jimmy sidled up to him and waited for an opening to say something. None came, so he broke in. "Hey, Bro," he said in a low voice, "let's head on out. I gotta be somewhere."

"Where's that?" Mort asked.

Jimmy leaned in and whispered, "Anywhere but here."

"Okay. I'll be right there."

Jimmy walked quickly to the front door and the safety of his truck. Mort turned back to Lila Ann, and they talked for a long time. So long that by the time they hugged and said goodbye, the kitchen clean-up had been completed, all the other visitors had departed, and Miss Mavis had disappeared. Jimmy had twice left his truck to peer into the living room window to see if his buddy was making any move to wrap things up.

෨෴෴

Finally on the road, Jimmy was happy to be looking at Miss Mavis' white columned house in the rear view mirror. Mort was happy, too. He was more than happy. On Cloud Nine, actually, thinking of Lila Ann and of driving up to Atlanta sometime soon to see her again.

Jimmy interrupted his reverie. "Your lady friend's a looker, man."

"Yes, she is,"

"You gonna see her again?"

"Yes, I am," Mort said confidently. As Jimmy turned onto Marsh Road, Mort observed, "You survived an hour of CBBS."

"Yes, Collier Bluff Bull Shit?"

"Now, James, that is not nice of you."

"Are they all like that?" Jimmy asked.

"All two that I have attended," Mort said.

Jimmy down shifted as he pulled into Maggie's drive. "Mavis kinda lost me with the stuff about the ants on the watermelon," he said.

Mort opened the truck door. "Thanks for the lift. You're picking me up now next Wednesday morning, right?"

"Yeah, right." Jimmy grunted.

"Well, at least you can look Jane Ellen in the eye and tell her how brave you were this morning."

Mort rounded the front of the truck and started for the front porch. Jimmy called to him. "Hey, how 'bout some fishing next week?"

"Maybe."

That night Mort waited for Weenie and Maggie to retire, then quietly snitched some of Maggie's bourbon and padded softly upstairs. Reclining against the old oak headboard, tumbler in hand, he once again delved into Uncle Steeney's little book. He opened it and reread the December 4, 1941 entry. He turned three pages to December 7:

The sun came up again today, steady and serene. But by now we are getting the news. God help Us all!!

Mort stared at the entry for a long time, then blinked and reached for his whiskey. He read five or six more daily entries, all from his birth year, 1948. He read each word, but the sentences didn't register. His thoughts and his heart were on his Georgia peach. He was smitten. Smitten hard.

Chapter 14

MORT HAD GROWN RATHER FOND of Maggie's garden bench. Not so much the bench itself. It was more the peace and quiet he had sitting on the bench, especially early in the morning before anyone else was up. This could have been such a morning, except that the serenity was marred by birds, probably Kamikaze Karl among them, that had splotched and splattered their white and brown and purplish-black loads on the newly painted bench. Mort stood over the bench, studying the situation. He went into the kitchen and returned with a paper towel. Unfortunately, the bird droppings were hard and dry and clung stubbornly to the bench seat. His one square of paper towel was no match. Reverting to his more customary work around problem-solving style, he went to the garage, fetched a can of paint and a brush, returned once again to the despoiled bench and proceeded to carefully paint over the birds' leavings. He stood back, judged his work to be satisfactory, and then retired to the swing seat on the front porch with his Roll Tide mug and newspaper.

As Mort sipped his coffee, his eyes caught the date under the *Collier Caller* front page banner: October 10th. His thoughts drifted back a few decades.

After he finished his twelve month tour in Vietnam, he had decided, instead of flying straight back to the States, to go to Taipei for a few days. After a solid year of ordering, receiving, distributing, and frequently consuming beer in the combat zone, he needed some time to decompress. It was not long after sunset in the Taipei's main square. Mort, caressing a large glass of vodka on the rocks, was seated alone at a small table at an outdoor café. His thoughts, like those of any soldier in his situation, were of relief to be away from war and finally removed from the threat of attack. But as he closed his eyes, anticipating the perfect joy that first taste of vodka would bring, all hell broke loose. Gunfire! The rapid rat-a-tat-tat of machine gun fire! Except for the night in Vung Tau when his army unit bulleted the tires of his tardy beer truck, this was the closest Mort had ever come to gun fire. He dropped his glass of vodka, spilling it entirely, and scrambled for cover under the tiny table.

The gun fire terrified him, but, in fact, it wasn't gun fire at all. Rather, it was a string of celebratory Chinese fire crackers. Happy Double Ten Day! October 10th in Taiwan. Double Ten Day, basically their Fourth of July, marked the founding of the Republic of China under Sun Yat-Sen.

Everyone in the square, except the cowering American soldier, cheered and sang. The shaken Corporal Boozer emerged from under his table and hailed a waiter to order two vodkas. The waiter struggled through his limited command of English. "You expecting friend?"

"No," Mort growled, "I am not expecting friend. I am expecting two vodkas. On the rocks."

The waiter probed again. "You want two—"

Mort held up two fingers. "Two vodkas, dammit!"

◈◈

His mind was still on that night in Taipei so many years ago, when Weenie stepped out onto the porch. "Morning," she said. "What are you doing out here?"

"Huh? Oh, just reading the paper."

"You never sit on the front porch," she said.

"Well, yeah—"

"Come on in for breakfast," Weenie said.

"Is Maggie up?" Mort asked, turning back to the October 10th edition of the *Caller*.

"Yes," Weenie said, "she's sitting out back in the garden."

Mort's head snapped up, eyes wide. "On the bench?"

"No, Mort. She's sitting in the bird bath. Yes, on the bench."

Mort mumbled and indecipherable expletive.

"What?"

"Nothing."

The trio convened for breakfast in the dining room. Mort sat at his usual place, hoping against hope that Maggie had somehow positioned her little hiney between newly covered bird poops. It was not to be. As Weenie slid Maggie's chair back for her, she exclaimed, "Honey, what have you got on your bath robe?"

Before Maggie could respond, Mort chimed in. "Oh, it's probably the white from back when Jonah was painting the bench."

"But it's wet," Weenie said, holding up a white index finger. "Look here."

Mort, trying very hard to sound nonchalant, said, "Well, Jonah probably came over this morning just to touch up the bench."

Maggie, who had no clue what the two were talking about, started to sit. Weenie grabbed her by the shoulders, catching her in mid descent.

"Don't sit down, dear!"

"What?"

"You'll get paint on the chair."

Weenie managed to relieve Maggie of her bath robe and headed into the hall. She was trying to decide what to do with the painted robe, when the phone rang. She called into the dining room, "I'll get it."

Mort buttered his biscuit and listened to his sister.

"Hello... ...yes, he's here.....who's calling? ... ...who? Just a minute."

Weenie, holding the bathrobe out at arm's length, stepped back into the dining room and looked at Mort. "It's for you. Some man. I didn't catch his name."

"What's he want?" Mort asked.

"He didn't say."

Mort reluctantly left his hot buttered biscuit and stood.

Maggie looked up. "You finished already, young man?"

Mort called over his shoulder, "No, Aunt Maggie. I'll be right back."

Weenie started toward the laundry room, but her curiosity over the mystery caller got the better of her. In the corner of the kitchen, back behind the front hall, she put her ear to the wall.

"Hello? Yes, it is—well, I'm not sure you've got the right Mortimer Boozer either, but there aren't many of us—what is it you want—okay, I'll listen."

Mort listened while Weenie listened to him listening. It was quite a while, the two of them listening. Finally, Mort spoke, "Is this a joke?" Then he backed off. "No, no, no—I understand," he said apologetically.

The caller was talking again. Mort said, "Well, I suppose. Let me think about it. Why don't you call me back in a few days—alright then—bye."

Weenie heard the telephone click into its cradle. She stepped away from the kitchen wall, looked down and saw white paint on her new pink Bermuda shorts. "Shit," she muttered.

In the laundry room, she took off her shorts and put them along with Maggie's bath robe in the washer. She went upstairs for a new pair of pants, then downstairs again to resume her breakfast. Maggie was still at the dining room table fidgeting with her empty coffee cup. Weenie sat and looked around. "Where's Mort?" she asked.

"Who?"

"The young man."

"Oh," Maggie said, contemplating the question. "I think he went outside."

Weenie peered out the window. Mort was sitting on the old log out by the river. "What's he doing out there?" she asked.

"How should I know?" Maggie answered. "Why don't you go ask him?"

"Good idea," Weenie said as she folded her napkin onto the table. In the kitchen, she emptied her coffee cup into a mug, topped it off and went outside.

Mort turned slightly as she approached. "Hey," he said softly.

"Hey to you." Weenie sat beside him. They both looked straight out at their old riparian friend. Weenie reached for a twig and tossed it into the river. She scanned the visible length of the river. "Where's Aaron today?"

"Not a clue," Mort said absently.

Weenie looked closely at Mort. "Are you okay?" she asked.

"Not really."

"The phone call?"

"Yeah."

"Care to tell me about it?"

"Sure," Mort said softly, then added, "I'm kind of in shock. Still going over it in my mind."

Weenie knew at times such as this it was best just to be still. He would share with her when he was ready. She watched two monarch butterflies as they bounced through the air along the muddy bank. The river, so quiet, flowed soft and smooth.

Mort broke into Weenie's reverie. "The call," he said, "was from a man in Missouri. I missed the name of the town. He said his name was Raymond Reilly."

"What did he want?"

"Said he'd like to come here to Collier Bluff and meet me." Mort took a deep breath and continued. "He says he thinks I'm his father."

Weenie unfortunately had just taken in a large mouthful of coffee which she proceeded to spray all over her clean, light blue Bermuda shorts. "What?" she gasped. Weenie wiped the hot coffee as best she could off her pants, her legs and her chin. "This man," she sputtered, "a total stranger in Missouri thinks you are his father?"

"That is correct." Mort answered flatly.

"Based on what?"

"Based on the fact or at least the assertion that Marcie is his mother."

"Your old girlfriend?"

"That's what he said. Marcie Pelham. The Marcie Pelham who suddenly dropped out of college and moved out of town."

"Oh my God," Weenie stammered.

"He also said he was born in St. Louis, and he told me his birthday. Sure enough it was about seven months after she moved away."

"So Marcie had him out in Missouri and raised him there?"

"No," Mort said, "she put him up for adoption."

Weenie looked down at what little remained in her mug and tossed it behind her. "How did he figure out the connection with you?" she asked.

"He didn't tell me that," Mort said.

"So maybe he just made it up," Weenie surmised.

"Why would he make it up? To inherit my vast fortune?"

"Good point," Weenie said. Then she asked, "When is he coming?"

"I don't know." Mort said, "I told him to give me a few days to think about all this and call me back."

They sat for a spell, side by side, just watching the river. Aaron came into view, flying low over the water against the current.

✥✥

Later in the morning, Weenie attended to Maggie's bathrobe. Fortunately for Mort, she had become so preoccupied with the bombshell news from Missouri that she forgot to pursue the mystery of the wet paint. Maggie, her mind meanwhile not preoccupied with much of anything, had retired to her bedroom to lie down for a bit before starting her day.

Mort drifted through his own day in a fog. Whatever his body was doing, his mind was on the phone call. He tried to reconstruct the man's exact words. When he wasn't replaying the telephone call, his thoughts were back four decades just before Marcie went back to college and before she vanished. After lunch, he walked back to the river and again sat on the log. He revisited that golden summer and their torrid encounters in the back seat of his dad's car and later, in August, at night on the beach in Destin, Florida. He worked the math again. Early June backwards nine months gets to—mid-August plus nine months is around the middle of—

That evening after Maggie and Weenie had retired, Mort slipped into the kitchen and quietly slid several large ice cubes into a tumbler. He then moved to the living room, silently filled the tumbler with Maggie's bourbon and tip-toed up to his room. In bed, he sipped the cool whiskey and reached for Uncle Steeney's diary on the night stand.

June 29, 1943 --- If God wants us to believe in him, why does he keep himself so vague? Like a ghost. It shouldn't be a game of hide and seek. And the Bible! If it really is the word of God, he's not a very good writer. Much too wordy. Too repetitive. I'm starting to think we've got the whole thing backwards. The world often looks scary, terrifying even, and back there always looming right behind us is our own inevitable demise. Solution? A supreme love and eternal life. And so, we all create our own gods. Problem solved.

Mort quaffed a slug and read the passage again. He then flipped ahead to a page more in the middle of the book.

August 19, 1945 --- The Japanese surrendered. Thank God, it's over! This damned war made me feel there is no God. The end of it makes me feel different. I can't embrace, and I can't let go. Driving me crazy!

Mort couldn't quite figure why he was drawn to the little book, but he was. He thought maybe it was that the entries were so short. If he didn't like one or didn't understand it or didn't agree with it, he could just pass through it and try another one, lickety-split. The bourbon on the rocks, now almost gone, had made the reading most pleasurable. Mort was tired from the day. He yawned and decided to read one last entry.

April 4, 1954 --- Great day in the morning! It has finally happened. My own sweet Ruth gave birth to our boy. Tears of joy in my eyes now. Past midnight, but I can't sleep. Never thought it would happen. Life comes at you quickly sometimes. I, we, have a son today! A son! I had given up. Ruth, too, I think. God, whoever or whatever you are, thank you! And let me please be a good and worthy father.

Mort reread the entry and looked at it for a long time. At last, he drained the tumbler, turned off the bed table lamp, and closed his eyes.

Chapter 15

"AHH," MORT PURRED WITH HIS eyes closed. "This is so smooth," he said holding the glass of bourbon in his hand and acting as though it had been a very long time since he had enjoyed the wonderful elixir. Maggie, during one of her increasingly unpredictable moods, had given Mort permission to have some of her Old Grand Dad.

It was cocktail hour at the old place, and it was All Saints day. Weenie offered a toast. "Here's to November, one of the best months in south Alabama. It's warm enough to be outside all day, and it's cool enough to enjoy it!"

Mort and Weenie raised their glasses, as did Aunt Maggie although she had no idea why she was doing so.

"Yes siree," Mort said, continuing to hold his glass aloft, "to the month of November. Definitely in the top twelve."

Maggie, confused as ever, looked at Mort. "What about an elf?" she asked.

Weenie patted her knee kindly. "Just enjoy your drink, dear."

Maggie looked down to her lap, seemingly surprised to find a glass in her hand.

Knowing her aunt couldn't hear her, Weenie whispered to her brother, "Poor thing. She's so frail now. She's lost even more weight, don't you think?"

"Yes," Mort whispered back, "she's almost skin and bones. I think just about the only thing left is her snarly attitude."

"Come on now," Weenie snapped. "That's not very Christian of you."

"Well, since I guess I'm not a Christian, I suppose you're right." The words were hardly out of his mouth when he regretted the jab. He sallied forth, hoping to soften the sharp edge. "Of course, I guess it was also rather un-Jewish of me and un-Buddhist and maybe even un-Druid, too."

Maggie perked up. "Fluid?" she asked. "What about fluid?"

Mort did not skip a beat. He raised his voice. "I said this bourbon is fluid. Isn't your bourbon fluid, Maggie?"

Maggie studied her glass. She swirled her drink and rattled the ice cubes. "Sure. Mine's fluid," she said.

Mort continued the goofy repartee. "Bourbon is good when its fluid, isn't it?"

But Maggie didn't respond. Her mind had drifted away to some distant ethos. Weenie, who had been a quiet witness to the strange interchange, looked impassively at her brother for a long time before declaring, "Mortimer, I love you, but you know, you really are an idiot."

Mort laughed. "Oh, and I love you, too, Roweena."

Weenie sipped her chardonnay and said wistfully, "I really do love November. The sky today was so clear and blue. Kind of cobalt. And quiet. Kind of like nature was finishing up with the summer and the heat and the blooming and is just getting ready for a winter nap." She paused to enjoy the view out the big bay window. "It is so peaceful right now."

And it was peaceful. Until the telephone rang.

"I'll get it." Mort put his drink aside and headed into the hall. He was on the call for a long time. Weenie strained to hear his end of the conversation, but was not having much luck. At the end, Mort signed off in a loud and declarative voice, one Weenie could hear fairly well. "Alright then, we'll see you down here in a few weeks. You've got my address and number. I've got your phone number—yes, you too—okay—bye."

Mort returned to the living room, sat down and reached for his drink.

Weenie looked at him, her eye raised brows saying, "Well?"

Mort took another ample slug of his bourbon and said, "That was the Missouri man. My quote unquote son." He took in more liquid fortification and added, "He wants to come visit. Said he's attending a conference in New Orleans and would like to drive over."

"When?" Weenie asked.

The telephone rang again before Mort could reply.

"What's going on here?" Maggie rasped. "This sounds like some kinda three ring circus."

"So far it's only two rings," Mort said over his shoulder as he jogged to the telephone. "Probably him again," he groused. He picked up the phone, talked briefly to the caller, returned to the living room, and said to Weenie, "It's for you. It's your daughter."

"Dabney? Really?"

Weenie scrambled to her feet and ran to the phone. It was a long conversation after which Weenie bounced happily back to the living room.

Maggie, her chin resting on her chest, was sound asleep which had afforded the opportunity for Mort to help himself to another drink. "And how is the young lady?" he asked.

"Everything's okay," Weenie said, beaming. "She's coming for Thanksgiving. Isn't that wonderful?"

"Wow," Mort said, pondering the news. "That's nice. That's really nice," he said and he meant it.

Chapter 16

A THIN SLIVER OF SUN, THE color of brushed bronze, peeked over the Hibiscus hedge. Mort again was up early, looking forward to some morning solitude. He puttered quietly in the kitchen with the coffee pot and the toaster. He was smoothing raspberry jam on his biscuit when it happened. No matter how many times it happened, each time was traumatic. From behind him, came the slamming whap of bird against glass. Kamikaze Karl was at it again. Mort knocked his biscuit on the floor. "Dammit!" He glared out the window. "You little prick," he whispered. "One of these days, I'm gonna nail your ass."

Mort moved as quietly as he could to wipe up the mess on the floor, hoping Weenie had not been roused. With his mug of hot coffee in one hand and the plate of biscuits in the other, he backed toward the old screen door, preparing to push it open with his rump.

Somehow the door opened all by itself just as Mort leaned his ass outward. With no resistance except from a cooling breeze, he fell backward on to the wooden stoop, and from there, down into an azalea bush. "What the hell?" he groaned. An invisible hand had pulled the screen door at precisely the right, actually the wrong, instant. It was the hand of Jimmy Claggett.

Jimmy looked down at Mort who had coffee all over his shirt and jam on his face and forehead. "Mornin', Bro."

Mort glared up at him. "What the fuck did you do that for?"

"I was just comin' in to say hello."

Mort struggled to his feet. "You ass-hole! Did you ever think to knock before coming in?"

"Sorreee." Jimmy bent down to pick up the shattered pieces of plate and Mort's prized Roll Tide mug which miraculously was still intact.

A second story window directly above them slid open. Weenie leaned out and scolded in a loud whisper, "What the hell are you two doing down there? Do you know what time it is?"

Mort looked up. "Yes, we do. It's time for you to go back to sleep."

Weenie studied the condition of her disheveled brother. "What's that on your face? Oh, my God! Are you bleeding?'

Mort put his hand to his forehead and looked at the red smear on his fingers. "Yeah," he said. He licked each of his fingers and then licked his lips.

"Oh, gross!" Weenie exclaimed as she lowered the window.

Mort and Jimmy took their seats on the garden bench with their coffees and a fresh batch of biscuits. Mort still had on his coffee soaked shirt, but had at least washed his face. "I'm really sorry, man," Jimmy said. "I didn't know you were coming out just then."

Mort replied through a mouthful of biscuit, "It's okay. You couldn't have timed it that well if you had tried." He savored his first taste of coffee of the morning. "What did you come over here for anyway?"

"Wanted to know if you'd like to go fishing," Jimmy said.

"Fishing? Today?"

Jimmy answered, "I know complex concepts are sometimes difficult for you, so I'll go slow here. I—thought—maybe—we—could—go—fishing—today."

"I don't want to go all the way down to the Gulf," Mort said. "The boat, all the gear."

"No, no," Jimmy said quickly. "The river. Just upstream a ways for catfish, maybe some trout."

Mort warmed to the idea. "Hmmmm. I'd have to change my shirt."

"Oh, well," Jimmy sighed, "I guess that's a problem then, isn't it? Why don't you check your social calendar to see if, besides changing your shirt, you have any other pressing commitments today?"

Mort chuckled self-consciously. He glanced at his old friend. Jimmy seemed different somehow. There was just the faintest hint of sadness in his eyes.

Five minutes later, as they were heading out the door, Weenie appeared with a box of bandages, Q Tips, and a bottle of mercurochrome. She stepped between Mort and the back door.

"Let me look at your face," she said. She pushed his thick bangs back off his forehead. "Well—what the—I thought you were cut," she said.

"I was," Mort said, employing his most serious tone of voice. "Pretty deep, too, almost to the bone. But I got down on my knees and asked God to heal me, and voila!"

"Well bully, bully for you. Glad you've finally see the light," Weenie said as she painted a bright red mercurochrome cross on his forehead and a large clown circle on the end of his nose. Mort wanted to swat Weenie's artistic hands, but his own hands were holding his rod and reel and tackle box.

"Going fishing?" Weenie asked.

Jimmy chimed in, "Very astute of you, Roweena. What was your first clue?"

"Going to the Gulf?" she asked.

"Naw, we're just headin' up the river a ways," Jimmy said. "We'll bring you some nice catfish."

☙❧

And they did. Shortly after noon, the two anglers returned with more fish than they knew what to do with. During their outing, Mort had told Jimmy about the phone calls from Missouri and that he wasn't entirely sure about the man's story, but that he might have a son and that the man from Missouri, who might be his son, was coming for a visit. Jimmy wanted to know who the mother was.

"You remember Marcie Pelham in our class?" Mort asked.

"Uh huh."

"That's her."

"Marcie Pelham? You're kidding!"

"That's what the guy said."

Later, while still upstream on the banks of the Monacoosa, Jimmy had his own news to share. Just as shocking. More troubling. He and Jane Ellen had just been told that Jane Ellen had cancer, serious cancer that had started in the lungs and had spread.

When Jimmy broke the news, Mort had just cast out to the middle of the river. Mort held his rod with one hand and put his free arm around his friend. "Oh, my God, man," he said, "I am so sorry." Mort wanted to say something more, but was at a total loss. He just clung to his friend's shoulder until Jimmy shifted to recast into the river.

His eyes were wet as he watched his tackle arc out over the water. "She told me to go fishing today," he said, swallowing hard. "Forced me, actually. Said she needed some quiet time. Said a little fishing would be good for me."

◈

Weenie turned into the drive as Mort and Jimmy were unloading their catch from the back of the red pickup. She parked, walked over to them and opened the big cooler. "Oh, my gosh. I've never seen so many! We can't eat all that."

"We're only taking half," Mort said.

"I know but even so," Weenie said, still staring down at the fish.

"Why don't you call Jonah and ask him if he wants some catfish,"

"Good idea,"

◈

After Jimmy left for home with his half of the catch, Mort set up his fish cleaning operation out by the river's edge. He heard a rustle of pampas grass along the shoreline and looked up to see Jonah's unmistakable straw hat bobbing above the bushes. Jonah came in to view holding a burlap bag in one hand and waving with the other. "Hi there, Mister Mort."

"Hey to you, old friend. Come for some fish?"

"Yes, sir, if you has any."

"I've got plenty," Mort said.

Jonah examined the filets already laid out on a large cutting board that was balanced on the log. He peered into the cooler to see what was still left to be cleaned. "Ooowee," he said, "you sho' got yourself a passel of catfish. Good size ones, too."

"How many you want?" Mort asked.

"Oh Lawd, Mister Mort."

"Take what you want. Really. I'm getting tired of cleaning these suckers."

Jonah pushed his hat to the back of his head. "How 'bout five. Is that too many?"

"Not too many at all," Mort said happily. "Pick the ones you want."

Jonah bent down, made his selections and slid them carefully into his sack. "Sho' is mighty nice of you. We'll have some fine eating tonight."

"Not at all," Mort said, relieved that his work load had been lightened.

Jonah looked kindly into Mort's eyes. Actually he was looking just above the eyes. "Mister Boozer," he said, displaying his wonderful big toothed smile, "am I seeing you have joined the fold here as a brother in Christ?"

Mort wasn't following this. Jonah only smiled more broadly and said, "Usually they are black or grey and folks usually have 'em just on Ash Wednesday. The red is kinda different, but it's beautiful."

Mort put his hand to his forehead. "Good grief. Why didn't Jimmy say something?"

"Excuse me?"

"Nothing," Mort muttered, still feeling his forehead with his fingers.

Jonah slung his sack over his shoulder and said, "Thank you so much. Genia is going to be so happy."

"You're welcome."

Jonah hesitated for a moment, and then said, "I know this is none of my business, but can I ask you something?"

"What is that, Jonah?"

Jonah pointed. "What's the red mark on your nose for?"

Mort put two fingers to the tip of his nose. "Oh, for God's sake!" He smiled self-consciously.

Jonah tipped his hat and turned toward the river. Mort rubbed his nose and forehead as he watched him step onto the path and disappear. At the back door, he plucked a couple of Scuppernong grapes and went inside.

Chapter 17

IN COLLIER BLUFF, IT WAS considered ill-mannered to go calling before nine in the morning, especially if one were visiting the infirmed. So Weenie stood on the front stoop of the Claggett home and checked her watch. Eight fifty-eight.

The house was small, but it was a charmer. Jimmy had built it himself, at least most of it. Stained wood siding, unusual for the region, clad the house. Two dormer windows protruding from the front roof. Jane Ellen's prized yellow roses bloomed all along the house on both sides of the front door.

The previous night, Weenie and Maggie had been treated to a meal cooked entirely by Mortimer Boozer. A culinary event so rare in its occurrence that Weenie had compared it to the Second Coming. Mort was so proud of the catch. He claimed most of the fish, or at least most of the big ones, had been caught by him. He insisted, therefore, on preparing the gourmet treat. *Catfish a la Mort*, he called it. Weenie, showing off her limited retention of high school French, cross translated it as *chat pesche of the dead*.

Regardless of the appellation, the meal—steamed fish, with collard greens, ochre and rice—was delicious. It was during dessert, peach ice cream, that Mort told Weenie the news about Jane Ellen.

"No!" Weenie gasped, instinctively placing her hand over her mouth.

Lucky for Mort that he waited until the ice cream to break the news. Otherwise, his culinary labors would have quickly become an afterthought. But now, of course, they did. As it was, Weenie raced through her dessert and relocated forthwith to the kitchen to prepare her signature zucchini and tuna casserole, of which she was most proud and which had been delivered unbidden to countless townspeople enduring hard times.

So now, she stood at Jane Ellen's front door, holding her casserole, waiting. At nine o'clock on the dot, she pressed the doorbell. The door opened immediately. It was Jimmy. Weenie moved in to give him a big hug, but the intervening tuna and zucchini prevented much of an embrace.

"Jimmy, I am so sorry to hear about Jane Ellen," Weenie said. "Do you think she might be up for a short visit?"

"She's out shopping," Jimmy said.

"Out shopping!" Weenie exclaimed.

Jimmy took a deep breath and touched Weenie's arm. "We got some bad news, but she's not dead yet, Weenie. We're going to go on about our lives as long as we can."

"Oh."

Jimmy relieved Weenie of her casserole and took it into the kitchen. They sat together on the living room couch. He recounted everything the doctor had told them, basically that the prognosis was not good and that Jane Ellen should start an aggressive regime of chemotherapy and radiation. They talked a long time, reminiscing about their high school days, their mutual friends and the multitude of odd twists and turns of their respective lives. Out of the blue, Weenie asked, "Why don't you both come over for Thanksgiving?"

Jimmy said he'd talk it over with Jane Ellen.

Weenie leaned over and gave him a long, close hug, and whispered, "I'll pray every day for both of you."

"Thanks," Jimmy whispered in reply. "That means a lot. It really does."

Jane Ellen pulled into the driveway just as Weenie was stepping into her own car. The women met in the middle of the front yard and embraced. Weenie was just about hugged out. She stood back. "You look really good!" she said.

Jane Ellen beamed. "You think I look good now, wait'll you see what I just bought." She reached into her shopping bag and proudly pulled out her new purchase. "This is for a little later," she said holding up a curly, page-boy red wig. "I always wanted to be a red-head." She laughed.

They moved to the front stoop and sat low on the step. An hour later, they were still talking and laughing and crying together.

Chapter 18

WEENIE HAD SET UP HER Thanksgiving Dinner Preparation Command Center in the kitchen and was busy supervising her staff which consisted of—herself. Two glass pie plates lay on the formica counter ready for the dough crust. A large can of cranberry sauce was next to a bowl of pearled onions that was alongside two bags of bread stuffing mix. Her mug next to the sink was full of coffee, now cold. Weenie had both hands in the dough bowl when she heard oyster shells crunching out front. She wiped her hands on her checkered apron, stepped into the dining room and peered out the front window. A car had pulled up close to the front porch. It was a silver sedan. Weenie looked closely. The car was parked at an angle from her vantage, and she couldn't quite read the license plate. She quickly retreated to the kitchen, removed her apron, washed and dried her hands, and smoothed her hair.

The doorbell rang. By the time she made it to the front hall, it had rung a second time. She opened the door part way. "Yes?" she asked.

He was a strapping fellow, dressed in a black suit jacket and black shirt. Deep blue eyes. A beard, an attractive one, dark brown, neatly trimmed. The truly arresting feature, the one that gave Weenie the shivers, was the narrow, white clerical collar.

"Hello," the man said.

Weenie caught her breath. There was fear in her eyes. She raised her hand to her cheek. "Hello," she said weakly. "Is this about Jane Ellen?"

"Who?"

"Jane Ellen Claggett?"

"Uhm, no," the man said, now as confused as Weenie. "I'm sorry, ma'am. Maybe I have the wrong house."

"Oh, I thought maybe you were here about somebody dying or something," Weenie said.

The man smiled. He had a very warm smile. "Well, we're all in the process now, aren't we?"

"Process of what?"

"Process of dying."

The conversation had taken a weird turn.

"Anyway, ma'am, I'm sorry I—"

Weenie interrupted him. "Well, who are you looking for?"

The clergyman cleared his throat and hesitated before answering. "I'm looking for a man named Mortimer Boozer."

"Mort?" Weenie said. "He's right here."

"Oh." The man shifted his weight from one side to another. "Is he your husband?"

"God, no," Weenie said, "he's my brother. That's bad enough."

The clergyman didn't know whether to laugh or run to his car as fast as he could.

"Come on in," Weenie said. "I'll get him."

Mort was in the back garden with his coffee and newspaper. Weenie opened the screen door and poked her head out. "There's a man here to see you. A minister."

Mort looked up. "A minister? What's he want?"

Weenie couldn't resist. "He says he needs to talk with you about your sins."

"Probably will be a long conversation," Mort said, folding his newspaper and laying it on the bench. He followed his sister into the house. Warily he stepped into the vestibule. "Hi," he said softly to the visitor.

"Hello," the man said. "I know I said I probably wouldn't be here 'til late in the day, but here I am."

Weenie had quietly slipped away and taken up her eavesdropping position in the living room.

"Excuse me?" Mort was asking.

The clergyman held out his hand. "I'm Raymond Reilly. We talked on the phone the other day."

A feather, even a very small one, could have flattened Mort. "You're Raymond Reilly?" he stammered.

"That I am," the visitor replied, smiling broadly.

"Wow!" Mort managed to say. "I'm just surprised."

"You mean that I'm here?"

"No. That you're a minister."

"A priest, actually," Reilly said.

Mort gulped. "A priest? Holy Mackerel!"

Reilly laughed heartily. "Yeah, the fishermen say that a lot in our order."

"Your order?"

"Yes. My order. I'm a Jesuit."

Mort had forgotten they had already shaken hands, extended his hand again, and again said, "Wow!"

"It's really good to meet you," Reilly said. "So, do you think maybe we could visit?"

"Sure. Sure, you bet," Mort said, unsteadily. "First, let me introduce you to my sister, Roweena."

Weenie appeared from around the corner on que. As introductions were being made, Aunt Maggie, barefoot and attired only in her flimsy night gown, wandered into the hall. The bearded priest was addressing his own aunt, saying, "It is so nice to meet you. You know, I have imagined this day for years and years." He paused for a moment, becoming a bit emotional. His eyes were moist. He swallowed, regained control, and added, "But here I am at last, right?"

Maggie's mouth dropped open. "You're here for Last Rites?"

Mort jumped in. "No, Maggie," he said.

"I'm not ready. No. Please not today," Maggie begged, her lower lip trembling.

Reilly, clearly befuddled by the old woman in the night gown, said, "I am really sorry to have come so early and unannounced. I apologize."

"I should say so!" Maggie growled. "You shoulda given me some warning."

Weenie reached for Maggie's arm and held it gently. "Honey, he's not here for you. This is Father Reilly from Missouri. He's here for Mort."

Maggie looked over at Mort. "Well, things are looking up now, aren't they?"

"No. No," Weenie said. "Not that. He is Mort's son."

"What?"

"Honey, Mort is this man's father."

Poor Maggie now was totally at sea. She looked over at the priest, then at Mort. She raised a gnarled forefinger in Mort's direction and asked, "He's the Father's father?"

"That's right, Hon," Weenie said, reassuringly.

"How is that so?" Maggie mused.

Mort said, "Aunt Maggie, we're not sure about any of this, just now. It's a very long story. I'll tell you the whole thing later."

Maggie, apparently forgetting the visitor had not come to perform Last Rites for her, said, "Well, you'd better tell me quick. I don't suppose I got much time."

The sound of crunching oyster shells out front heralded the arrival of another visitor. A car door opened and slammed shut. Rapid footsteps thumped up to the front porch. The second early visitor opened the screen door for herself. "Hey, y'all. Happy Thanksgiving!"

It was Dabney arriving from Memphis. She was, as her mother occasionally commented, "ever so slightly plump." She possessed that unusual combination of naturally blond hair and brown eyes, and her naturally blond hair was also naturally curly. Her full lips were quick to form into a wide smile. She made a bee-line for her mom and gave her a hug. "It's so good to see you," she said. She turned and held her arms open wide. "Hey, Uncle Mort." Another hug. "It's been such a long time."

"Sure has," Mort said, putting his arms around her.

As Dabney turned toward the owner of the home, Weenie said, "Honey, you remember your great Aunt Maggie, don't you?"

"I sure do," Dabney replied, giving Maggie a peck on the cheek.

"You here for the Last Rites?" Maggie asked.

Weenie broke in, saving Dabney from having to figure out what in the world her great aunt was talking about. "Dabney, I want you to meet Father Reilly."

"How do you do, Father," she said, as they shook hands. She looked up into his marvelous blue eyes a bit longer than she should have. She snapped herself out of her momentary trance. "Do you live here in Collier Bluff?" she asked.

"No," the priest said, still holding her hand. "I live in Missouri. I'm just visiting."

"Oh, are you having Thanksgiving with us?"

Reilly, a bit taken a back, was getting ready to answer no, but he never got the chance.

"Oh, yes, "Weenie gushed. "That would be great. Absolutely! You should join us."

Before Father Reilly had a chance respond, the matter seemed to be settled. Mort stared at his sister, trying to figure out what had just happened.

So it was that for the first half hour of Raymond Reilly's momentous encounter with his long lost father, he had ventured no further than two feet inside the front door. Finally, Weenie decided to take Dabney upstairs to get her settled her into a guest bedroom. Mort suggested to Reilly that the two of them move to the garden to talk. That left Maggie, standing barefoot, alone in her night gown in the middle of the foyer, wondering if she had just entered the After Life and, if so, why it looked so much like her old house.

☙❧

Mort and possible son sat, a bit awkwardly, side by side on the white bench.

"Do you go by Raymond?" Mort asked.

"Ray, actually. Please call me Ray." When Mort had asked if he would like anything to drink, Ray said, "I think maybe the occasion warrants a cold beer, if you have one." Mort readily agreed and thought it would be bad manners not to join the priest in drink. He loped to the house and returned promptly with two cold ones. Ray proposed a toast to their meeting. "To our meeting," he said.

"You bet," Mort said.

They clinked cans.

Mort savored the cold brew, then suggested, "So why don't you fill me in with some more background about yourself and how you found me?"

"Okay. I guess I should start from the beginning,"

"Not a bad plan," Mort said, as he settled back on the bench, took another long, slow drink and prepared himself for the story.

"As I think I told you when we talked on the phone," Ray began, "I was born in Ladue, a suburb of St. Louis." The saga proceeded apace to his placement for adoption with a private agency to joining, at the age of eleven weeks, the Reilly family in Jefferson City, Missouri. June and Jeff Reilly, both strong, committed Catholics, already had a four year old adopted daughter. Ray moved more slowly through his upbringing in the family and his attendance at parochial elementary school and high school. He graduated from Notre Dame with a major in history. "After graduation," Ray said, "I spent the next two years in West Africa with the Peace Corps. I came home with no idea what to do with the rest of my life."

"I know that feeling," Mort said dryly.

Ray continued, "So I just went back to Jeff City and lived with my parents for almost a year. It would have been longer except my dad eventually told me I had to get out of the house and do something."

"I know that feeling, too," Mort said.

"Oh, really?" Ray was apparently intrigued enough to detour from his own story. "Your dad told you to go do something after college?"

"After high school," Mort said.

"Oh, and what did you do?"

"I joined the Army and went to Vietnam."

"Wow!" Ray said. "Did you see a lot of combat?"

"Oh yeah," Mort lied. "Lots."

"Really? Tell me about it."

"Another time. Let's finish your story."

"So anyway," Ray resumed, "I made two important decisions around that time. I decided to go into the priesthood and I also decided to find, or at least try to find, my birth parents. I entered seminary that fall, but I didn't act on the second decision, at least not for a long time. So I became a 'man of the cloth' and started my service. But the idea of finding you guys and learning where I came from—" Ray paused. "It was sort of an odd loneliness. Kind of like a low grade fever that just wouldn't quite go away." He uncrossed and recrossed his legs. Then he held his now not so cold beer to his lips. But he didn't drink. "Last year, I started to search. First, I contacted the adoption agency," he said. He walked Mort through his investigation. After the agency, he contacted the Missouri Bureau of Vital Records where he saw, for the first time, his pre-adoption birth certificate with his birth mother's full name: Marcia Lane Pelham

"And have you met her?" Mort asked.

"I have," Ray said. "It took me a while. I found out she lives in Kansas City. Got her address and wrote her a letter. She didn't reply for the longest time. But finally, she did."

"And?"

"And we met. Had a very pleasant visit over lunch. She's nice. Married. Has two grown children who I'm hoping to meet also."

Mort gazed up through the magnolia branches to the morning sky. "Well, I'll be damned," he whispered.

Ray finally gave himself permission to drink some of his beer. "She told me about you. About you and her, and she said she has always felt badly about not letting you know."

Mort looked down, slowly tapping his empty can on the bench between his legs. Then he stood. "I'm going to get another beer," he said. "Want one?"

"No thanks."

As Mort walked toward the house, his son called after him. "She said if I met you to please give you her regards."

Mort nodded and disappeared into the kitchen.

Back in the garden, Mort took his seat and started in on his own second beer. "I hope you don't think I am unfriendly or unappreciative about your visit here," he said. "I'm not at all. Just still a bit overwhelmed by all this." He looked directly at Ray. "I want you to know I am glad you came and I'm looking forward to us spending time together."

Ray was visibly relieved at Mort's change of demeanor. "I'm so glad to hear you say that. My stomach has been full of butterflies all morning." He smiled a wide, happy smile. "I'm looking forward to our time together, too." He took a deep breath and added, "You know, when Marcie first told me about you and that you were from Alabama, I thought maybe I was connected to one of those legendary Southern families like Beauregard or Ravanel or Butler."

"Butler?" Mort asked.

"You know, Rhett Butler."

"Oh, sure," Mort dead-panned. "Big southern name."

Ray sighed. "Sadly," he said, "I guess it was just not to be."

Mort said brightly, "Yes, but just think how lucky things turned out for you."

"Lucky?" Ray replied.

"Sure," Mort said. "You could be going through life as Father Boozer!"

"You're right!" Ray agreed. "That would be a fate worse than death. By the way, I sensed you were caught off guard when your sister invited me for Thanksgiving. I really don't want to interfere."

"Oh, no, no. Please stay. You've come all this way," Mort insisted, "You definitely should stay."

"Well, if you're sure it's okay."

"It's absolutely okay." Mort stood. "Let's go inside now and get you settled in your room."

As they walked together toward the house, Mort touched Ray's shoulder and said, "By the way, my buddy and I are going fishing in the morning. Why don't you come with us?"

"Fishing?"

"Yes. Fishing. You know with a pole and a hook?"

"Well—"

"Come on, it'll be fun. You might catch a holy mackerel."

Chapter 19

WEENIE WAS MANNING THE BARRICADES at her Thanksgiving Dinner Command Center and she was not happy. Her checkered apron was splotched with a variety of half-prepared food samples. Both of her cheeks, just below two glowering eyes, displayed smudges of dough and baking powder. Mort held his half-consumed glass of orange juice waist high. "I was thinking," he said sheepishly, "that Jimmy and I would go to the Gulf and go fishing. Just for the day."

Weenie glared at him, speechless for a moment. She wagged a dripping wooden spatula at her brother and barked, "It's the day before Thanksgiving! We have house guests. Jimmy's dear wife is dying of cancer and you two are going down to the Gulf to go fishing! What are you thinking?"

Mort responded, "Also, I was thinking maybe we could bring back some fresh fish for the dinner tomorrow."

Weenie angrily waved her outstretched arm across the counter. "Turkey, Mort. We are having turkey for Thanksgiving!"

"I know, Weenie. Of course. I just thought maybe you could stuff the turkey with some red snapper or maybe grouper."

Weenie was very near the end of her rope. "Fish is not on the menu tomorrow. Period." She then pivoted to another subject. "So let me get this straight now. Your long lost, unknown son, your closest living relative, has come all the way from Missouri to meet you and you are simply going to leave him here with me all day?"

"No, of course not," Mort said, blandly. "He's going with us."

As if on cue, the kitchen door swung open and in stepped the good priest. "Good morning, everybody," he said in a cheery voice. "I'm all ready, Mort."

Mort and Weenie regarded Ray with quiet astonishment. He was attired in his clerical collar and black shirt that was tucked neatly into a pair of Mort's multi-colored, but ripped and very faded, Madras shorts. A rope belt held the oversized pants in place. The eclectic ensemble was finished off below with calf-high black socks and black dress shoes. Ray looked at Mort and Weenie. "What?"

"Nothing, nothing at all," Mort managed to say.

The sound of crunching shells signaled the arrival of Jimmy with his truck, trailer and boat.

Mort said to Weenie, "Okay, hon. I guess we'll be going now."

"Don't 'hon' me. Leaving me here to do all the work."

Ray tried to placate her. "Maybe we'll bring back a nice fish to serve tomorrow."

Mort jumped in. "No! No! We just went through that."

Weenie desperately needed a break from her turkeys, the one she was related to and the one she was preparing to cook. She headed out of the kitchen, pushing the swinging door into the dining room. Unfortunately, Aunt Maggie was once again on the other side contemplating her next move in life. Roweena thumped the old lady who proceeded to cry out and fall backward. Fortunately, Maggie's trailing four legged companion softened her fall. Seymour yelped and whined. Maggie screamed and then glared up from the floor. "Goddammit! Why'd you do that?"

The two men raced into the dining room and knelt alongside Weenie and the ailing and very angry old woman. Mort looked at Seymour. He was tempted to shift his care to the whimpering hound, but didn't dare. Maggie, now a veteran of swinging door attacks, was miraculously only shaken up. She was in sufficient condition to swear mightily and curse, especially at Mort, who she was certain had perpetrated the attack. Once it was clear the old lady was relatively alright, Mort and Ray beat a hasty exit toward the front door.

Mort called over his shoulder, "See ya. We'll be back later."

Ray, trailing behind his father, called back to the dining room, "I'll pray for you, Aunt Roweena."

Weenie, holding Maggie by elbow, hollered, "You'd better pray for your father that I don't kill him when he gets back."

"Okay," Ray called from the hall.

Weenie sang out a second time before the fishermen could complete their escape. "Mort, take that damned dog with you."

The boat launch resembled a second episode of *Keystone Cops Go to Sea*. A priest with his black shirt, white collar, and torn Madras shorts, sitting in the middle of the boat facing aft. A one-eyed hound, having his most exciting day in a dog's memory, was poised at the bow like a proud masthead on an ancient sailing ship, pointing like the trained hunting dog he was not. Mort, nervously holding on to Seymour's collar, with the tense expression of a man who was not yet having fun, which he was not. Captain Jimmy, his Atlanta Braves baseball cap on backwards, was steering the boat, pleased with himself that he only had to whack Quirky Merky once to bring her to life. Shortly after getting underway, they had to return to the dock twice, once for Jimmy to fetch his dark glasses and a second time for Ray to take a pee.

But compared to their last offshore venture, this one was starting off relatively smoothly. As they motored south toward Dauphin, the priest marveled at the gliding pelicans, the squawking seagulls, and a lone dolphin breeching close by on their starboard side.

Jimmy decided they would try their luck off the eastern tip of the island. Arriving at the chosen spot, he cut the engine. They drifted with the current as Mort and Jimmy baited hooks and prepared two of Jimmy's prized rods and Mort's only rod. Seymour paced and whined in excited anticipation, probably with little notion of what it was he was anticipating, only sensing that whatever it was it would be exciting. Mort handed a rod to Ray who took it and held it like a baseball bat. Mort kindly provided a tutorial on the finer points of holding and operating a rod and reel. They settled in to "catch the big one." Seymour had quieted and, except for the gentle lapping of water against the boat and the occasional cawing of a bird, it was deliciously serene for a few minutes.

Jimmy, who bored easily, soon became more interested in conversation than serenity. "So Father," he said, "I am sure you are a skilled fisher of men. Are you a fisher of fish, too?"

"Ah, Jimmy, I gather you have a familiarity with Scripture."

Jimmy chomped a large divot out of a shiny red apple. "Oh, yes," he said, "I am quite devout."

Mort's mouth dropped open. Seymour, lying on the floor boards, lazily opened his one eye.

Jimmy continued, "Yes, siree. I go to church a lot. Especially on Sundays."

Mort began to reel in. "You know, Jimmy," he said. "Lyin's a sin. You'll go to Hell for that. Isn't that right, Ray?"

"Well, actually—" Ray began.

But Jimmy was on a roll and interrupted. "You know, Father, your son here doesn't believe in Jesus." He took another bite of his apple.

"Jimmy, stop it!" Mort snapped. "We've talked about this. Now cut it out."

Ray looked at his father and raised his eyebrows. "Is that true, Mort?"

"I tried to explain this to my dufus friend here the last time we were fishing."

Ray looked from Mort to Jimmy and back again. "And what, if I may ask, did you explain to him?"

Mort took a deep breath and exhaled. "So I think Jesus an all-around good guy," he said with slow deliberation. "He was a great teacher. The best. But you know, I just think that—"

Jimmy interrupted for a second time. He had set his trap and Mort had gone right in. "Oh my god!" Jimmy exclaimed, looking behind Mort out in the distance. "Look at that black storm cloud!"

Mort froze. "What?" His voice trembled. He turned around, knocking his rod against the gunnel, losing it in the water. The sky off to the west was a cloudless Robin's egg blue.

Jimmy collapsed in uncontrolled laughter.

Ray looked back and forth between the two as if he were watching a tennis match. But unlike tennis, he had no idea what he was witnessing.

Mort glared at Jimmy. "You ass-hole!"

Jimmy eventually got himself under control. After a deep gasp of air, he chided Mort one more time. "Hey, bro, are you aware your rod went overboard?"

"Yeah," Mort said. "Doesn't bother me a bit."

"Oh, you're such a stoic."

"No, really. I don't care."

"Come on."

"Why should I care," Mort replied calmly. "It was your rod."

Jimmy's devilish delight vanished. "What? You bastard!"

Jimmy spat, cocked his arm, and hurled his partially eaten apple at Mort. Unfortunately, the good priest, sitting amidships, was in the captain's line of fire. The rocketing fruit splatted into Ray's ear. Jimmy leapt to his feet to attend to his unintended target. "Oh, Father, I am so sorry!"

At the same time, Mort, taking umbrage at the attack on his ostensible son, grabbed a handful of cut squid and hurled it at Jimmy.

❧❧

Hours later, while driving back to Collier Bluff, each maintained a different version of events and a different assignment of blame. They were, however, of one accord in their memory that all three men wound up overboard, clinging to the side of the boat, while Seymour, the only living creature left on board, barked orders from the bow. Following considerable flailing and cursing, all were able to clamber back into the boat.

After his first ever dip in the Gulf of Mexico, Ray had reclaimed his seat amidships, removed his wet collar, his shirt and shoes and socks.

Wiping his face, he turned to Mort. "Is this a typical fishing outing for you guys."

"Unfortunately, it's starting to feel like that," Mort said.

They sat in their wet underwear and fished for an hour. That is, Jimmy and Ray fished. Mort, being without pole, entertained himself by scratching Seymour behind the ears and discussing the nature of the Man from Nazareth with his newfound son. Jimmy chomped on a fresh apple and fished in sulky silence.

By mid-afternoon, the sun was well into its autumn descent toward the southwest horizon. The wet clothes were almost dry. The day's catch consisted of three good sized red fish and two grouper, amazingly all caught by the rookie from Missouri. Jimmy, slowly getting over his funk, spoke admiringly to Ray, "Your first time out? I can't believe you caught all those fish!"

"Well," Ray grinned, "you know God rewards the righteous."

After another hour with no bites, Jimmy fired up old Merky on his first pull and turned the boat toward the Alabama mainland. A fiery sun touched the sea as they docked.

⊗⊗

A pale light of a three-quarter moon shafted through the high branches of the grand old magnolia as Jimmy pulled up to Maggie's front porch. On the drive home, Mort had tried, without success, to persuade Jimmy to take the fish.

"Nah. Ray, you caught 'em. You keep 'em," Jimmy had protested. "Okay, guys, here you are. Another memorable outing with Mortimer Boozer. Ray, glad you could join us."

"You bet," Ray said.

"And I'm really sorry about the apple I threw."

"I know," Ray said.

"I'm not sorry I threw it. I'm sorry it hit the wrong person," Jimmy said.

"Don't think a thing of it," Ray said. "We are to forgive as the Lord forgives us."

"Yes, we are," Mort said. "I forgive Jimmy for trying to injure me with a fruit missile. Ray forgives Jimmy for actually hitting him. Jimmy forgives me for losing his fishing rod. I forgive Jimmy for scaring the shit out of me with the fake storm. And God will hopefully forgive Father O'Reilly for selfishly not allowing anyone else to catch a single fish. So we're all square?"

"All square," Jimmy said. "See you tomorrow. Three o'clock?"

"Three o'clock," Mort confirmed.

The red pick-up rolled slowly out of the circular driveway. Mort left his gear and the cooler of fish on the porch and opened the front door for Seymour, who had just returned from doing his business out by the river.

The house was quiet. The big dining room table was all arranged, place settings for nine. Ray stood next to Mort in the foyer wondering what was next on the agenda, hoping whatever it was involved sleep. It was not to be.

Mort whispered, "We gotta clean the fish before we go to bed."

"Clean the fish?" Ray whined in a whisper.

"Well, they're not gonna clean themselves."

Seymour quietly padded toward the kitchen to inspect his bowl. Mort followed him. Seymour examined and sniffed his empty bowl and looked up with his one eye and a mournful expression. Mort, of course, didn't want to be bothered searching for the dog food. He retrieved two raw hot dogs from the fridge, cut them up, letting the pieces fall into the dog's bowl and topped them off with a large dollop of butter pecan ice cream. Seymour happily devoured the concoction and loped upstairs to Maggie's bedroom.

In the meantime, Mort got busy setting up his fish cleaning station on a card table he had carried out to the garden. The table was illuminated by a pole lamp he had taken from the living room and plugged into an extension cord that he had run from an outlet in the kitchen and out a window next to the coffee maker. He laid a fish on the table and the remaining four in waiting side-by-side on the white bench.

"You've really never cleaned a fish?" Mort asked.

"Never. Really," Ray answered.

"Well, watch and learn from a master. It's a fine art and takes a very special talent."

Mort pushed his sleeves to his elbows and brought the lamp pole closer to him. Like a maestro holding his baton motionless before commanding the first note, Mort held his scalpel above the fish. The dramatic pause—and begin. He deftly made a vertical cut, severing the tail from the body. He then fingered a spot right behind a gill, inserted the knife, removing the head.

Ray took a deep breath and continued to watch intently as Mort scraped the head and tail off the edge of the table into a metal bucket.

"That's pretty simple," Ray said.

"We're just getting started," Mort said as he turned the fish on its back, sliced open the belly and buried his hand inside. The hand emerged with a ghoulish tangle of slimy intestines, mucous and blood.

Ray recoiled. "Oh, my word!"

"Oh, come on, Father. It's just part of God's wondrous creation."

"I know," Ray said weakly, "but it just seems so—"

"It's a good thing you didn't decide to become a surgeon," Mort reached back into the fish, excavating more guts that he splatted into the bucket. He began stroking the side of the fish against the grain with his scaler, peeling off the rows of translucent scales. When he was sure all scales had been removed, Mort laid his finished product on the garden bench and picked up the next in line. "Okay, your turn," he said.

Ray pleaded. "Me? Can I just watch you do one more?"

Mort laughed and turned his attention to Fish Number Two. The moon was high. A light nocturnal breeze flowed in off the river. Ray watched Mort slice the tail from the body. Mort, his head still bent down toward his task, said, "I've been thinking about our talk this afternoon."

"Our talk?"

"You know. In the boat. About Jesus and stuff."

"Oh, yes. Sure," Ray said. "What about it?"

The fish head came off and was scraped over the side into the bucket.

"I was just thinking," Mort said, "you told me that I shouldn't worry too much about Jesus and who he was—is."

"Right," Ray said.

Mort looked up at him. "Are you sure you're a priest?"

"Yes, Mister Boozer. Quite sure."

Mort punched the point of the knife into the rear end of the fish's belly and sliced it open. He gathered a fistful of guts and held it nonchalantly between his own gut and Ray's and said, "So you're saying that it's okay if I have doubts about Him and all that?"

"Oh, Mort, it's natural. We all have doubts. Even our Lord had doubts. He had doubts that night in the Garden of Gethsemane and he had doubts on the cross. 'Oh, God, why hast thou forsaken me?' he prayed that night. We mortals are not supposed to know everything. Adam, remember, got himself in a fix when he ate from the Tree of Knowledge."

Mort, still holding his dripping wad between them, asked, "Are you saying that if I don't believe Jesus is divine, I'm not going to Hell?"

Ray, turning to avoid looking at the fish guts, answered, "As I said, we mortals are not supposed to know everything. I sure don't have all the answers. But what is the problem with not knowing with certainty?"

"Well," Mort said hesitantly, "I guess I just want clarity."

"Of course you do," Ray agreed. "It's human nature. But think for a moment. Let's say you had the definitive answer about God. Would you love your family any more or less? Would the sky be any bluer? Would life be more worth living?"

Mort pondered those questions for a long time, responding finally, "Yeah. Maybe not."

Mort finished up with the gutting, wiped his hands on a paper towel and reached for his scaler.

"But I will tell you one thing I know for sure," Ray said, "and this is in Scripture. If you force a priest against his will to gut and clean a fish, you will definitely go to Hell."

Chapter 20

T HANKSGIVING DAY IN COLLIER BLUFF. Early morning sunlight glistened on dewy grass. The sky was a cloudless blue, the air delightfully still, and it was a serenely quiet morning until—

"Mort!"

Weenie's tense fingers gripped the foyer bannister post. She shouted up the stairs again, "Mortimer Boozer!"

Mortimer Boozer was uncharacteristically sleeping in. All the driving the day before, the fishing, the theological jousting, and the late night fish cleaning had plain tuckered him out. He struggled to sit up in bed. He rubbed his eyes.

"Mort, we have a crisis!" Weenie shouted again, "Get your ass down here!"

Turns out, it was a crisis Mort himself had created the night before. After Ray went to bed, Mort packaged and stored the cleaned fish. He then returned to the backyard and uncoiled the garden hose from the garage to wash down Maggie's treasured bench, the card table, and his cleaning instruments. Unfortunately, in the process, he sprayed the pole lamp which sparked and flashed before knocking out power in the house. It was late, and he was very tired. He would handle the problem in the morning.

Now it was the morning. Weenie was not happy. "Mort!"

This final outburst was so loud even Maggie heard it. Maggie stumbled out of her room and onto the second floor landing. "What in tarnation!" she wailed.

Weenie looked up. "Will you tell Mort to please get down here?"

Mort, donned in plaid boxer shorts, appeared next to Maggie on the upper landing. "Hold your horses," he said. "I'm coming."

He stepped barefoot onto the foyer. "What is this crisis?" he asked.

"My problem, dear Brother," Weenie snapped, "is that I am trying to cook a Thanksgiving dinner for nine people and there is no damned electricity in the house. Will you please do something quick?"

"Ah, no power," Mort mused. He rubbed his chin in Sherlock Holmes-like fashion. He was now awake enough to recall the events of the previous evening. "I think I know the problem," he said.

"You do?" Weenie asked, incredulously. "How do you know the problem? You just woke up."

"I have a hunch," Mort said. "I'm good at stuff like this."

He padded to the hall closet, found a flashlight and headed into the basement in search of the fuse box.

Meanwhile, Weenie fretted, drumming her fingers on the kitchen counter. There was a sharp knocking on the swinging door. "Yes?" Weenie asked.

"Are you coming out?" It was Maggie from the dining room.

"Coming out?"

"Yes."

"No."

"Okay. I'm coming' in."

Maggie pushed the door. Seymour preceded her and headed for his bowl.

"Morning,'" Maggie grumped, heading for the coffee pot. "How come it's so dark in here?"

Weenie sighed. "It's not a good morning."

"Whatsa matter?" Maggie asked.

"I can't cook because there's no electricity."

Weenie had hardly finished her sentence when the overhead light went on. She gazed up to the light as if she were seeing the Angel Gabriel. "Hallelujah," she whispered.

Mort emerged triumphant from the basement. "All fixed," he said nonchalantly, putting the flashlight back in the closet.

Seymour inspected his empty bowl then sidled over to Mort, nuzzled his leg and looked up at him with one longing eye.

"What made the power go out?" Weenie asked.

"I have no idea," Mort lied. "These things just happen sometimes."

Weenie, greatly relieved and cheery, gave Mort a big hug and a peck on the cheek. "My hero!" she gushed. "For an idiot, you really are smart sometimes."

"Thank you, sis," Mort said, "and by the way, I can count, too."

"Oh?"

"You set nine places at the table."

"Correct," Weenie said.

"There's only going to be seven of us."

"No, nine," Weenie said.

"Seven," Mort asserted confidently and proceeded to count off on his fingers "You, me, Maggie, Jimmy and Jane Ellen and Dabney and Ray."

"And Jonah and Eugenia," Weenie added.

"Jonah and Eugenia? Who invited them?"

Weenie sighed and said, "Maggie invited them."

Maggie, examining the cold, empty coffee pot, turned around. "What'd I do?" she asked.

"You invited Jonah and Eugenia here for Thanksgiving dinner."

"No, I didn't."

"Yes, you did."

"I did not."

"Well, they're coming," Weenie said with finality.

Mort worked his way to the far side of the kitchen to make the coffee. "Well, this'll be a Thanksgiving to remember," he said.

A mellow afternoon light slanted through the dining room windows and sparkled Maggie's crystal goblets. Eight, each with plate in hand, were queued by the sideboard. As they inched by the steaming turkey, the gravy boat and the side dishes, Weenie stood apart smiling at the fruits of her labor. Except for Maggie, who Weenie helped into her customary chair at the head of the table, the rest sat where they chose. Dabney, decked out in her finest frock and ruby red lipstick, a bit too much lipstick, maneuvered to sit next to the handsome priest. Jonah and Eugenia sat together next to Maggie. Jimmy and Jane Ellen worked their way through the buffet line with Jimmy holding and filling plates for both of them. Jane Ellen had lost weight and moved with a cautious deliberateness, but her eyes were bright and her smile was wide. Her red wig, perched high atop her bald head, looked rather goofy; but she obviously didn't care, nor apparently did anyone else. Mort, last in line, plopped a final large dollop of mashed sweet potatoes on his plate and took a seat at the far end of the table.

Finally, Weenie filled her own plate and sat next to Mort. She took her fork and clinked it on the side of her water glass. All eyes turned to her. "I am so glad we could all be together today," she said. "It just makes Thanksgiving so special. Jonah and Eugenia, you have been with us so long you kind of feel like part of the family. And Jimmy and dear Jane Ellen, it is wonderful to have you." She paused, giving Mort the erroneous impression he could start eating. Weenie, smiling to the group, elbowed him sharply as he tried to get his fork into some turkey. She continued more loudly, "And, Maggie, we thank you for allowing us to all be together with you in your home."

"You bet," Maggie said, looking uncertainly around the table. The old aunt then raised her water glass and said, "Merry Christmas." To which the rest raised their glasses and dutifully repeated, "Merry Christmas."

Mort reached for his fork and received another jab from Weenie who turned, still smiling, to Ray, and asked, "Father, would you mind saying a blessing for us?"

"Of course," Ray said. He bowed his head and reached for hands on either side of him. Except for Seymour's soft snoring under the table, the room was silent. Ray began, "God in Heaven, we give thanks on this special day for all our blessings and for the bountiful harvest of the season. Though we are miserable sinners in your eyes, we beseech you once again to forgive us and to allow us to walk in Your light. We ask all of this, oh Lord, in the name of Your Son, Jesus Christ. Amen."

And all around the table chorused, "Amen."

Mort released the hands on either side of him and grabbed his knife and fork. His utensils were poised over plate ready once again to strike, when another piece of silverware clinked another crystal glass. It was Ray again.

"I hate to keep your pallets waiting much longer, but if you will forgive me." He cleared his throat and swallowed. "I want to thank you all, especially the Boozers here, for allowing me to be with you. I have been waiting a long time to meet my birth father and the family, waiting with both eagerness and fear. Eagerness for closure and fear that I might not be welcomed. Fortunately, that fear, so far, has proven to be unfounded. Although I must say, when we first met," Ray nodded in the direction of the foyer, "the father, realizing he was with the son, looked like he was seeing the Holy Ghost!"

Mort winced, then smiled wanly. Everyone else laughed.

Ray raised his glass. "And so, I want to offer a special toast to my father and to the Boozer family and to all of you."

All glasses raised again. "Hear. Hear."

And Mort, finally, was able to get a piece of now lukewarm turkey onto his fork and into his mouth. Everyone else dug in as well and, for a minute, the only sounds were those of silverware softly scraping on plates.

The telephone rang. Weenie pushed back her chair and walked to the hall as she asked of no one in particular, "Who's callin' in the middle of Thanksgiving dinner?"

"Just let it go," Mort suggested.

Weenie ignored his advice and answered the phone. She returned and said, "Mort, it's for you"

Mort looked up. "Can you tell him I'll call back?"

"It's not a him, and she said she'd only take a minute."

Jimmy figured things out before Mort did. "Oooooh," he teased, "I'll bet the call's from Atlanta. Might be your Georgia peach."

Mort blushed as he rose to take the call. Contrary to Lila Ann's assurance that she would only take a minute, the call was quite long. In fact, Jonah and Jimmy had almost finished their second helpings by the time Mort returned. He sat, put his linen napkin in his lap and stared at the white patch of table cloth where his plate used to be. "Where's my dinner?" he asked.

"I'll get it," Weenie said. "I put it in the oven to keep it warm for you."

Eugenia said, "Miss Roweena, everything is just so delicious."

"Why thank you," Weenie said as she disappeared into the kitchen.

Jonah meanwhile tried to engage Maggie in conversation. "Miss Maggie, I saw you out in the garden the other day."

Maggie looked at him through her glasses. "You saw me what?"

"In the garden."

"You were in the garden?"

"No, you were in the garden."

"No, I wasn't"

"The other day."

"The other day?"

"Yes," Jonah answered patiently. "You were sitting on the bench."

"I suppose," Maggie said flatly. "Don't really remember."

Jane Ellen began a new conversation, mercifully rescuing Jonah from the dialogue that was heading nowhere. "Father," she asked across the table, "how long are you able to stay with us?"

Ray held up an index finger while he chewed and swallowed. "Pardon me," he said. "I have to leave very early Saturday morning to drive my rental car back to New Orleans and then fly to St. Louis. I have Mass on Sunday."

Weenie was back at the table. "Oh, I wish you could stay longer," she said.

Dabney perked up. "Why, I'm leaving early Saturday too. Driving back to Memphis." She turned to Ray. "St. Louis is right on the way. Why don't you ride with me?"

Weenie said, "Honey, you said you weren't leaving until Sunday."

"No, I didn't," Dabney said, frowning.

Mort interrupted his eating long enough to say, "St. Louis is not on the way to Memphis."

"Why it surely is," Dabney said petulantly. "At least the way I go."

Ray said, "That is mighty nice of you, but I have a rental car to take care of."

128

But the ditzy daughter was not to be denied. "We can return it right in Mobile. I can just follow you. It's right on the way."

It was Mort's turn again. "Mobile from here is not on the way to St. Louis which is not on the way to Memphis."

"Oh, come on," Dabney pressed. "It'll be fun. I never even knew I had a cousin 'til now. We can talk and get to know each other."

"Well, I'm not sure just how—" Ray fumbled about with the idea, not realizing his new found cousin had made the decision for him.

Weenie had returned to the kitchen and emerged with her pumpkin pie and a large bowl of whipped cream which she placed proudly on the sideboard. "Okay ya'll," she said proudly, "please come for some pie and let's move into the living room."

Folks rose from the table. Jimmy sidled over to their hostess. "Weenie, Jane Ellen's getting pretty tired. I think I'd better get her on home."

"Oh, I wish you could stay," Weenie said softly, "but I understand." She gave Jimmy and Jane Ellen each a big hug. "I'll come over real soon, and we can have a relaxing visit."

As the Claggetts said their goodbyes, Weenie moved in to help Maggie stand. "Let me get a piece of pie for you. You go on into the living room, and I'll bring it in."

"No, thanks," Maggie said, steadying herself with a hand on the table. "I'm going to bed. Want to get ready for Santa Claus."

"It's Thanksgiving, Maggie."

"Thanksgiving?"

"Yes."

"Well, I'm still going to bed," Maggie said, heading to the stairs.

Seymour emerged from under the table and looked around, clearly torn between following his mistress and staying put amidst all the good smelling food. He sniffed and whimpered, then drooped his head and followed Maggie up the stairs.

Chapter 21

IT WAS VERY FOGGY THE following morning. Weenie, Mort, and Ray stood together on the big front porch. Weenie, still in her bathrobe and slippers, cradled her coffee mug in both hands. Ray stood next to her, dressed in his priestly togs. Weenie blew gently over her mug, looked up at him and said, "I sure wish you could stay longer. Seems like you just got here."

"I know," Ray sighed. "Don't know where the time's gone. It's just been the most wonderful time. You all have been so nice."

Mort turned back toward the front door and called in loudly, "Dab, you'd better get a move on. Ray's gonna leave without you."

Dabney answered from upstairs, "I'm coming. Just give me a minute!"

Maggie had not yet made an appearance, but her four legged emissary was in the foyer, his nose pressed against the inside of the screen. Mort opened the door for him. Seymour stepped out, sniffed a few legs, then negotiated the big wooden steps to the lawn and disappeared into the fog.

Dabney called plaintively from the second floor landing. "Could someone maybe help me with my suitcase?"

"I'll help her," Ray said, handing his mug to Mort.

He bounded up the stairs, took Dabney's heavily laden suitcase in hand and began his descent. Dabney followed behind with one arm holding her hanging clothes and the other clutching her purse, her electric hair dryer, and her wide brimmed straw bonnet with a bright pink and baby blue ribbon. And then it happened. Her heel caught on the second step causing her to fall forward onto Ray who in turn also fell forward. Fortunately, Ray let go of the suitcase and was able to grab the bannister with both hands. Dabney managed to stop her own fall by letting go of all her paraphernalia and throwing her arms around Ray's neck and her legs around his waist. The suitcase, which sprung open, the purse, the electric hair dryer, and the straw bonnet with the pink and blue ribbon all cascaded loudly down the stairs.

"Oh, my God!" Weenie screamed. She and Mort dropped their mugs and rushed into the house. They stepped around the debris at their feet and stared up at the dazed priest with the arms and legs of a dizzy dame tentacled around him.

"What happened?" Mort asked.

"Are you alright?" Weenie added.

"I'm so sorry," Dabney wailed as she gingerly lowered herself off of Ray and grasped the bannister with both hands. "It's my fault," she gasped. "I slipped on the step."

As Ray and Dabney made their way cautiously to the bottom of the stairs, Maggie appeared on the upper landing. She stared down at them and at the debris in the foyer and at Weenie and Mort who were staring back at her. "What in hell are you people doing? And in the middle of the night!" Maggie said.

"It's alright, Maggie," Weenie said. "They just had a little accident on the stairs. Everybody's okay."

"I don't care about them," Maggie snapped. "I don't even know them. What about my house?"

"Nothing's damaged," Mort said,

Dabney chimed in, "Aunt Maggie, I am so sorry about this." She pointed to Ray. "It wasn't his fault."

Maggie scrutinized the scene below her. "That minister there. Was he comin' up to see me? Comin' for Last Rites?"

"No, Maggie," Weenie said reassuringly. "He's been visiting us, remember? He's Mort's son that has come from St. Louis."

"Mort's son?" Maggie queried. "Mort's the Father's father?"

"Yes. Mort is the Father's father. Now why don't you get dressed and come on down and say goodbye."

"Say goodbye? Where am I going?"

"No, Maggie. Ray and Dabney are leaving. Come on down."

Dabney's belongings, minus the hair dryer, the shattered pieces of which were tossed in the garbage, were gathered, repacked and placed in her car. Ray's single small suitcase lay in the back seat of the rental car. Even though Ray was going to be driving at least to Mobile, Mort offered him a strong slug of Maggie's bourbon to steady his nerves. The priest readily accepted.

Everyone was now gathered on the porch. A pale sun emerged through the thinning veil of fog. Seymour also emerged from the fog and joined the group which was busy laughing and chatting their goodbyes. Mort touched Ray's arm and lightly guided him to the far end of the porch. He put his hand on his son's shoulder. "I just wanted you to know how much all this has meant to me," he said.

"Well, and to me, too, for sure," Ray said. "Unless someone is an adoptee, it's hard to describe the experience." His eyes glistened. He swallowed hard, then continued, "This means so much. I hope we can stay in close touch."

"We will. I promise. You are welcome anytime," Mort said.

Ray gave Mort a big, long bear hug and whispered into his neck, "May God bless you."

"I still don't understand who the heck He is, but I'm thinking I'm already blessed." Mort said.

Ray and Dabney descended the porch steps very carefully and got ino their respective cars. Dabney rolled down her window, leaned out and called to Ray. "Follow me. I know where the rental car place is in Mobile."

She started her engine and flipped on the head lights which illuminated two shadowy figures coming out of the fog right in front of her. It was Jonah and Eugenia. They walked around to the side of the lead car and leaned in. "Miss Dabney," Eugenia gushed, "we was hoping you wouldn't be gone before we could come say good bye."

Ray turned off his engine and got out of his own car to shake Jonah's hand. And Weenie and Mort and Maggie and Seymour all came down off the porch and they proceeded to do all their hugging and goodbying all over again. By the time the two-car caravan finally moved out toward Mobile, the fog had all burned off and the sun shone brightly all over south Alabama.

Chapter 22

AS FALL SLID TOWARD WINTER, happy hour at the old house started a bit earlier each week. It wasn't yet five o'clock, but the indigo twilight outside was already fading to grey.

Maggie, attired in one of her nicer calico dresses, sat in her customary chair by the side table. Seymour snored lightly, his head resting as usual on Maggie's foot. Weenie and Mort flanked the big hearth in their own usual seats. Weenie turned to Maggie and said with a loud voice, "Mort laid a fire in the fireplace. Shall he light it for us?"

Maggie's dull eyes sparkled ever so slightly as she crooned in a raspy voice, "Come on, baby, light my fire."

"My word," Weenie exclaimed, "where did that come from?"

Maggie kind of smiled.

Mort said, "I think maybe she heard it on the radio earlier in the kitchen."

Weenie laughed. "Okay, brother, you heard the lady. Go ahead and light her fire."

Mort knelt in front of the hearth and set the screen off to one side. He struck a match under crumpled newspapers and sat back in his chair. He raised his glass. "Cheers. It's Pearl Harbor Day. A toast to all of us veterans."

Maggie, holding her glass of bourbon with both hands, raised it shakily. "Cheers," she said.

Weenie followed suit, "Cheers," then added with a dramatic flair, "and to our own brave veteran here. Speaking of which, Mort, why don't you tell Maggie about your courage under fire back in Vietnam?"

"Oh, no," Mort protested. "I don't want to go there. My PTSD might flare up again.

"Oh, you're right, of course. How insensitive of me," Weenie said. "I'll tell then."

Weenie faced Maggie, leaned in toward her and raised her voice again. "So one day our very own Corporal Boozer here was driving an Army truck with important military supplies and the enemy was waiting for him. In fact, they had been waiting a long time and they were kind of pissed. So Corporal Boozer rolled into an ambush, and the enemy shot all the tires out from under his truck." Weenie took a sip of her wine and continued her tale in a loud voice. "The corporal miraculously escaped death and delivered vital supplies to our troops." Weenie paused again, this time for dramatic effect. "Isn't that something?" she asked rhetorically.

Maggie agreed that it was, indeed, something.

Mort drank his bourbon and muttered, "I never should have shared that story with you. It's gets a little weirder each time you tell it."

The story just told was long gone to Maggie. She stared blankly into the dancing flames of the fire. At length, she blinked and brought herself back to the room. She glanced down at the glass she still held with both hands. She looked up at Weenie, then over to Mort. "I just want to tell you two that I've been kind of ornery lately. I know and I'm sorry. You both been good to me, and I appreciate it."

Weenie and Mort glanced furtively at each other. Weenie said, "Maggie, we appreciate you so much. You have been so nice to let us stay here."

Well," Maggie rasped. "It's better'n being alone." She looked over at Mort, adding, "A little better anyway."

Mort stood up and said, "On that cheery note, let's all have another pop."

Weenie held out her empty wine glass for him. While he worked the bar for himself and his sister, he said, "Why don't we all go out together in the morning and get a Christmas tree?"

"Great idea," Weenie said.

Mort handed Weenie her wine and extended his hand to Maggie. She looked up at him. "What?"

"Would you like a little more bourbon?"

"No, thanks," Maggie answered, "I'm real tired right now. I'm going up to rest for a bit."

Weenie asked her to be sure and come back down later for dinner, but she knew she wouldn't.

⊗⊗

The dawn honking of Canada geese over the house woke Mort. An hour later, the sharp thwap of the *Collier Current* landing on the front porch woke him a second time. This time, he rose, dressed and quietly padded down stairs. He brewed coffee, put two slices of bread in the toaster and went to the veranda for the newspaper. He stood on the porch for a moment, gauging the weather. Yes, he thought, with a sweater, it's warm enough, though just barely, to sit outside. He returned to the kitchen and repaired to the back garden, laden with coffee, buttered toast, and the newspaper. The garden bench was covered with sheen of dew, but he sat anyway. He turned first to the last page of the *Current*. Mort always said that the fact that the obituaries are invariably more interesting than the front page tells you all you need to know about life in Collier Bluff. He had finished his toast and coffee and was finally turning to page one when Weenie appeared with her own coffee and toast. She sat beside him. "Good morning."

"Good morning, m'lady," Mort said, scanning the front page for something he didn't already know.

Weenie sipped and chewed in silence, taking in the day. "Sleep okay?" she asked finally.

"Uh huh." Mort gave up on page one and circled back to the sports section.

Weenie said, "Wasn't that interesting last night what Maggie said about us?"

Mort looked up. "It was interesting," he said genuinely. "It really was."

"You know, if we're going to get a tree, we'd better get her up."

"Aw, let her sleep. We've got time," Mort said.

Weenie yawned and looked absently out toward the river and the wide marsh beyond. Aaron was pecking and poking at the water's edge along the far bank.

"Let's take a walk," she suggested.

This surprised Mort. He looked up and considered her offer for a moment. "Sure, why not?"

For almost an hour, they strolled the path along the river, chatting in the crisp December air, talking easily about nothing in particular and, for the first time in a long time, simply enjoying being together.

The morning was no longer young when they stepped off the path and back on to Maggie's yard. They both saw Seymour pawing at the back door trying to get back in to the house.

"What's with the old hound?" Mort asked.

"Maggie probably let him out and can't hear him'"

"Or maybe he pushed the screen door and got out himself."

Seymour turned his one eye on them and bounded toward them. Mort bent over and boxed his ears. "Hey, buster, whatcha doing? Maggie locked you out and you want your breakfast, huh?"

The dog ruffed and whined and turned back toward the house. "Okay, you old hound," Mort said, "we'll get you in."

"He's acting kind of strange."

"Yeah, a bit," Mort agreed opening the screen door.

Weenie stepped into the kitchen and surveyed the room. No fresh coffee had been made. She called out, "Maggie, you down here?" She waited. "Maggie?" she called as loudly as she could. Weenie said to Mort, "Get Seymour some food. Let me go see what she's up to."

Mort, still clueless as to the whereabouts of Seymour's food, filled his bowl with Raisin Bran and topped it off with two raw eggs. The dog was in heaven. Mort poured himself some orange juice, leaned against the counter and took in the view outside. Wild ducks flew out over the wide marsh beyond the river. A grey cloud bank had gathered in the west beyond the marsh. A cold rain was coming. He finished his juice. Seymour licked his empty bowl and sniffed the near environs for any errant morsels.

Mort looked again at the gathering storm. Behind him, he heard the soft creaking swing of the kitchen door.

Weenie entered the kitchen. She slowly placed her hands on the counter. Her lower lip quivered. She looked up at Mort. "She's dead," she said softly.

Weenie fell against her brother's chest and cried. Mort folded his arms around her and nuzzled her hair. He looked one more time out at the serenely flowing Monacoosa. Large, cold rain drops streamed from the sky and pelted the window.

Chapter 23

MAGGIE WAS TO BE LAID to rest on the winter solstice. Wisps of somber clouds scudded over the First Baptist Church of Collier Bluff, while inside the church, a modest klatch of mourners gathered in the front pews, the majority of whom were loyal members of the women's Bible study group. Miss Mavis, solemn and dignified, sat in the front pew. Mort, also in the front pew, was wedged between his sister and Lila Ann who had driven herself down from Atlanta that morning. Jimmy and Jane Ellen, more frail than ever, sat directly behind them along with a smattering of other friends and town folk.

The organist concluded the final prelude selection and Reverend Stephens stood, raising his arms out wide. "Please rise. Hymn number six twenty-two."

Weenie reached for a hymnal which she and Mort could share. As the organist began, Rose Jamison reached forward from the second pew putting her hand on Weenie's shoulder, and whispered, "This was Maggie's favorite."

I danced in the morning
When the world was begun
And I danced in the moon
And the stars and the sun.

It was during the singing of the last stanza that Weenie's eyes widened in sudden recognition. She leaned up to Mort and put her lips against his ear. She whispered over the music, "Incredible, huh?"

"What?" Mort whispered back.

"The song."

"What?"

"This song." Weenie whispered insistently. "The dance man. This is Maggie's dance man!"

> *Dance, then, where ever you may be.*
> *I am the Lord of the dance, said he.*
> *And I'll lead you all where ever you may be*
> *And I'll lead you all in the dance, said he.*

"I'll be damned," Mort muttered between stanzas.

> *I danced for the fishermen*
> *For James and John*
> *They came with me*
> *And the dance went on.*

The singing concluded and the congregants took their seats. Reverend Stephens walked to the pulpit and ascended the five steps. He once again stretched wide his arms and addressed the gathering in a fulsome baritone. "Dearly beloved, we are gathered—"

He was interrupted by a scuffling commotion at the back of the church. Two late comers noisily pushed open the big door. One of the two exclaimed, "Oh dammit, I left the flowers in the car." Dabney, wearing her straw hat with a wide blue and pink ribbon, was clearly discombobulated. She looked up, embarrassed to see that most of the congregation had turned around and were looking back at her. Ray sheepishly closed the door behind them, took Dabney's elbow and guided her to a seat.

The reverend cleared his throat and started again. "Dearly beloved, we are gathered here today to celebrate the life of Magnolia Dabney Boozer Paxton, a proud citizen of Collier Bluff, a daughter of the South and a humble child of God."

It had been years since Maggie darkened the door of the church, and it was clear from the reverend's very hazy homily that he really didn't know her. But he waxed on eloquently about the virtues of the deceased and at one point said, "Magnolia was a truly wonderful lady, so gentle, so demure and kind."

This prompted Weenie to reach for Mort's hand, not as a gesture of tenderness, but as a preemptive strike to head off any snide, whispered comment. Mercifully, Mort held his tongue. Jimmy, however, could not contain himself. From the second row pew, he leaned forward between Weenie and Mort and whispered, "Are you sure we're at the right funeral?"

Mort snorted. Weenie whispered back angrily, "Hush!"

The reverend concluded his homily by reading a final note in the program. "Immediately following the service, Maggie will be interred in her garden at her home. Family members only." The congregants then lined up in the center aisle for their wine and wafer, returned to their pews and rose for the final hymn, number one forty-six, "Gladly, the Cross I'd Bear," coincidentally a hymn of great significance in the young years of the Boozer siblings. Memories flooded back in a gusher for Weenie about the cross-eyed bear named Gladly and how big brother would tease her unmercifully by crossing his eyes, raising his hands as bear paws, and glaring down at her.

It was toward the end of the second stanza when Mort turned toward Weenie, raised his claw-like configured fingers to his shoulders, crossed his eyes and stared down into her face. Weenie, still singing, looked up at him and totally lost it. Fortunately, the booming sound of the organ partially muffled her hysterical outburst and convulsive laughter. When Mort pantomimed a second time, Weenie handed her hymnal to him, knelt, and buried her face in her arms. Her laughter, to all but Mort, seemed a wail of sorrow.

The final verse of "Gladly, the Cross I'd Bear" concluded, and the congregation began to leave the church. Miss Mavis quickly closed her own hymnal and maneuvered to Weenie's side. She slung her beefy arm around her, murmuring, "Oh, Honey, I know it's so hard." Miss Mavis turned to Mort, "Poor thing. Is she going to be all right?"

"I think so," Mort dead-panned. "That last hymn was pretty grizzly for her though." This tipped Weenie into another bout of hysterics which prompted Miss Mavis to throw both of her beefing arms around her which, in turn, prompted additional ladies of the Bible group to huddle around to comfort her.

Finally, composure was restored and Weenie, along with the others, gathered outside and began to mingle and talk. The low clouds had finished their scudding and a weak winter sun appeared.

Weenie was engaged in conversation with a Bible study member. Mort came up behind her and said, "Let's skedaddle. We gotta make sure everything is ready at the house."

Mort felt a large hand on his shoulder and turned. "Excuse me. Mister Boozer?" the owner of the large hand said. The man was stocky, youngish, with a thick shock of blond hair and matching, bushy mustache. "I'm sorry to interrupt," he said. "My name is Perry Blevins. I'm a lawyer here in town. Could I possibly have a quick word with you and your sister?"

Mort sized up the stranger for a moment. "I thought I knew all the lawyers here," he said.

"I grew up here," the lawyer said, "but I've been working up in Birmingham. Last year I moved my practice back to Collier Bluff."

Mort studied the man's face. "Are you by any chance related to Roy Blevins?"

The man smiled. "That's my dad."

Mort shook his hand and interrupted his sister's conversation. "Hey, Weenie, this is Perry Blevins, Roy's son."

Weenie smiled. "Hello. We knew your father in high school here."

"Nice to meet you, ma'am," "Blevins said. "I know you have to be off to the burial, but I wanted to talk with you both for just a minute."

"That's about all the time we've got," Mort said.

"I'll be brief, I promise," Blevins said. "I wanted to let you know that I represented Miss Paxton. She came with a lady friend of hers to see me a few months ago and asked me to help her prepare a will."

Weenie and Mort glanced at each other. Blevins continued, "You are both mentioned in the will. In fact you, Roweena—may I call you Roweena?"

"Most people call me Weenie," she said.

Blevins blanched. "Weenie?"

"Yes, Weenie, "she said. "Like the hot dog."

Mort added helpfully, "And also like the—"

"Mort!" Weenie snapped.

"Well, okay," Blevins said. "Now where was I?"

"You were asking if you could call me Roweena, and I said—"

"Oh, yes," Blevins said, brightening, "Miss Paxton, in her will, named you as executor."

Weenie put her hand to her chest. "Me?'

"Yes."

"What am I supposed to do?" Weenie asked.

The lawyer said, "Why don't both of you come by my office tomorrow or whenever. I can show you the will, and we can discuss how to proceed."

He pulled out his wallet and handed Mort a business card. "Call my office if you would and set up a time convenient for you all to come by."

∾∾

Brother and sister, with Lila Ann trailing close behind, hustled up the front porch steps and into Maggie's house. Weenie said, "We've got to get things ready quick. The others will be here any second."

"Okay," Mort said.

"Can you and Lila Ann get the bar set up? I'm going out back to make sure everything's ready to go. Do you think Jonah is still here?" Weenie asked.

"Beats me," Mort said.

Weenie, being Weenie, had it all planned out. The little group would stand behind the white bench while Ray would say a blessing and, being a clergyman, add anything else he wanted to. Weenie would then lay some flowers on the grave, they would all sing "Rock of Ages Cleft For Me" and then go inside to the living and open the bar.

145

Weenie walked quickly to the kitchen, opened the screen door, stepped out, surveyed the scene before her—and froze. Her mouth slowly fell open. Jonah was sitting on the garden bench wiping his sweating brow with his red and black handkerchief. A shovel rested upright against the back of the bench. Behind him, midway between the bench and the old magnolia tree was a large freshly dug rectangular hole and beside the hole, a large mound of dirt. Seymour wandered slowly around the grave, sniffing and poking. Jonah wiped his face again and looked up. "Good morning," he said wearily. "I's not quite done. Ran into some tree roots, and they been giving me a dickens of a time."

Weenie was speechless, but finally managed to mutter, "Tree roots?"

"I'm really sorry. I just—"

Weenie turned toward the house and bellowed, "Mort, come out here! Now!"

Moments passed. Mort stepped outside and warily approached his sister. Weenie, struggling to contain herself, asked, "What did you ask Jonah to do here?"

Mort glanced past Weenie at Jonah. "I just—" he stammered, "I told him to dig a hole between the bench and the tree for Maggie."

Weenie glared fiercely at him. "And did you happen to mention Maggie had been cremated and that the hole should be about the size of a COCA COLA CAN?!"

Mort backed away. "Well, I must have—"

"Brother," Weenie exploded, "you are without a doubt the dumbest man in Alabama! You have a lot of competition for that title, but you have won hands down!"

Mort backed away as Weenie advanced, her stare piercing into his guilty eyes. He took another retreating step, bumped into Seymour, knocking the dog into the grave. The poor one-eyed hound landed at the bottom of the hole yelping and whimpering. Jonah leapt to his feet. He and Mort lowered themselves down and wrestled Seymour out of the hole.

Weenie meanwhile plaintively raised her eyes to the heavens, beseeching, "Oh, Lord God, please, please deliver me from this idiocy."

Mort hoisted himself out of the grave and offered a hand to Jonah. He turned to Weenie. "All I can say, Sis, is I am very, very sorry."

Weenie took a long, exasperated breath. She turned to Jonah. "Well, look, I hate to ask you to do this, but please put the dirt back in the hole."

෨෩

The Claggetts and Ray and Dabney arrived together in Jimmy's truck. Dabney opened the front door and called out, "Hey, y'all."

"In here," Lila Ann answered from the living room.

"Where are Mom and Uncle Mort?" Dabney asked as she turned the corner.

"They're out back getting things ready," Lila Ann said.

The foursome went back to the kitchen and stood in a row studying the odd scene out the window. Weenie and Mort were standing under the magnolia tree engaged in some sort of animated discussion. Jonah was bent over furiously shoveling dirt in the hole. Seymour, off to one side, was bent over licking his hind leg.

"Gosh, I guess we're late," Jimmy said softly. "Looks like they've already buried her."

Lila had taken it upon herself to make a drink for everyone and, sensing that the hostess was preoccupied out back, decided further to go ahead and serve them. With a tray of glasses of straight bourbon encumbering both hands, she pushed open the kitchen door with her rump. The foursome turned away from the window. "Hey, guys," Lila Ann chirped. "Something here to wet your whistle."

Ray hesitated and said, "Shouldn't we maybe wait just a bit?" But before he could finish his sentence, Jimmy and Dabney had each grabbed a glass. The remaining two hesitated, but not for long.

Dabney downed a healthy slug of her bourbon and exclaimed, "Oh, shit, I left the flowers in the car again," and marched double time to the front door. She returned, a bouquet in hand, and looked around the kitchen for a container. Fortunately, a vase just the right size was just in front of her on the counter.

Weenie came in to the kitchen from outside. "Okay," she said. "We're ready."

"Hey, Mom," Dabney interrupted.

"What," Weenie snapped, anticipating another problem.

"I just noticed," "Dabney said, gesturing toward the window. "You've got this bird feeder here on the inside. Isn't it supposed to be—?"

"Yes, Dabney," Weenie snapped, "bird feeders are normally on the outside so the birds can actually feed. Talk to your nutty uncle about it later. Come on now, we've got something a little more important to attend to."

The little group filed out to the garden, and Lila placed her tray with the two remaining drinks on the bench. Except for Jane Ellen, who, due to fatigue, sat next to the bourbons on the bench, everyone stood solemnly around the now filled-in grave.

Earlier, after Jonah had filled the hole and wiped his beaded brow one last time, he waved goodbye and turned toward the river path and home. Weenie and Mort called after him and urged him to remain for the service. "Maggie loved you so much, Jonah," Weenie said kindly. "I think it would mean a lot to her if you stayed."

Jonah seemed a bit puzzled by this and was clearly exhausted, but obliged.

Now he stood leaning heavily on his shovel handle, staring wearily over at the white bench wishing his tired body could be sitting on it.

Everyone bowed their heads for a moment of silence. Ray glanced over at Weenie for the go-ahead nod to proceed. She nodded. He started. "We are gathered here at this special place—"

"Excuse me," Lila Ann interrupted. "I'm so sorry, but I just noticed we all have a drink here except poor Jonah who has done so much hard work."

Jonah protested, but Lila Ann persisted. "No, please," she said. "It's rude not to offer everyone the same. I'll be back in a jiff." She ran to the house and returned with another glass of bourbon on ice. "Here you are," she said, reaching across the grave and handing the glass to Jonah.

"Thank you, ma'am," Jonah said, drinking half the glass in one thirsty gulp.

Ray once again looked to Weenie for a go-ahead. She nodded, and he began again. "We are gathered here at this place—"

"Oh, my God! Wait!" It was Weenie this time who interrupted.

"What?" Ray asked.

"I forgot Maggie."

"Maggie?" Ray said.

"The urn. Her ashes," Weenie exclaimed as she dashed to the house. In the kitchen, her eyes darted frantically searching for the urn. She missed it the first time around the room, but part way on the second lap, she locked in on Dabney's flowers that were in the urn. She clenched her teeth to stuff a primal scream. She flung the flowers in the sink and headed back to the gravesite, urn in hand. She stepped back into her previous spot, holding the urn. It seemed to her heavier than before.

Ray didn't bother getting the nod this time. "Okay," he said. "Let's try this one more time. We are gathered here at this special place to be in spirit with a special friend and, for some of us, a very special relative." He continued with additional warm sentiments about Maggie and nature and God and Jesus and about how they should all love and be kind to one another. All the while, Weenie was holding the heavier-than-before urn, glaring menacingly at her daughter.

Ray finally wrapped up his somewhat disjointed homily, saying, "—and now we will gently deliver Maggie to her final place of rest on earth."

Jonah's last task before the service had been to create a small hole in the center of the fresh fill dirt. As Ray read some burial liturgy from a small black book, Weenie stepped forward to pour Maggie's ashes into the small hole. But Dabney had added water to her flowers in the kitchen, so the remains of poor old Magnolia Dabney Boozer Paxton oozed out as grey sludge.

"Oh, yuck!" Dabney gasped.

Weenie glared at her, shooting piercing darts from her eyes. Part of Maggie clung stubbornly to the inside of the urn. Weenie raised her hand to tap the bottom of the urn as one would do with a ketchup bottle, but quickly dropped the idea. Instead, she calmly placed the urn itself into the small hole as far as it would go, which was not all the way. Jonah, with no prompting, gently covered the top of the urn with several shovels full of earth. Weenie stepped back and wiped tears from her eyes.

Ray closed his little book and looked around uncertainly, deciding finally that it was probably up to him to say something. This, he remembered, from his seminary days, is what his professor had called "clerical improv." "Well," he said, "this might seem like the burial from hell, but I can assure you that Miss Maggie is in heaven right now. May the grace of the Lord be with her and with us all."

With that, folks started to move away from the grave. Mort then said, "Uhm, before we go inside, I'd like to say something."

The group reluctantly edged back toward the grave. Mort cleared his throat and looked down at the fresh dirt. "I guess I just want to get something off my chest. I don't think Maggie liked me too much and, to be honest, she wasn't my favorite person in the world. She could be a little, well, you know, rough around the edges, and I poked fun at her from time to time." He coughed and cleared his throat. "But really she was kind-hearted and, for the past three years, she let Weenie and me live here. For free. And I am very, very grateful for that. She was a good, good person, and I only wish I had had the sense to say that to her when I could have." Mort said all this while looking at the grave. Now, he raised his head and looked at the group. "That's all I wanted to say." He concluded, "Let's go inside and see if there's any bourbon left."

Everyone followed Mort's suggestion except Seymour who sniffed around Maggie's grave one last time then wandered off toward the river.

Chapter 24

I N THE LIVING ROOM, MORT lit the fire he had laid early that morning and settled into his customary wingback chair. As the flames danced and crackled, he raised his glass. "Cheers."

The internment of Aunt Maggie, disastrous as it was, was mercifully behind them and Weenie, for a while at least, no longer had to be in charge of planning or managing anything. Her mood, consequently, had brightened considerably. She and Mort laughed uproariously as they recounted their childhood kerfuffle over Gladly, the cross-eyed bear, Mort's ghoulish impersonation that morning, and Mavis' earnest efforts to ease Weenie's anguish.

Another round of drinks and a snack tray of cheeses, chips, and guacamole was offered and accepted by all. Mort stood and placed another log on the fire. Lila Ann, addressing no one in particular, said, "I really liked that hymn we sang this morning."

"Which one?" Jimmy asked. She proceeded to sing softly, "Dance, dance wherever you may be."

Weenie chimed in, "Rose told me in church that was always Maggie's very favorite hymn. Who knew? I'll bet Rose asked the church to include it in the service."

Mort rose to stoke the fire and said, "Maggie was always muttering about the dance man and we never knew what the heck she was talking about."

Dabney wiped a spot of guacamole from her chin saying, "I think we missed the first song."

"Yes, you did," her mother said, unsmiling.

"So who's the dance man, anyway?" Dabney asked.

"The dance man from the song," Weenie said.

"I know that," Dabney retorted with a slight edge, "but who is he?"

Weenie responded. "If one pays attention to the lyrics, I think it is pretty clear the dance man is Jesus."

"I don't think so," Jimmy said. "He's just like a general spirit."

"That's not right, Jimmy," Weenie admonished. "Go read the lyrics."

Mort turned to his son. "Ray, you're the resident expert here. What say you?"

Ray put his glass and plate on a side table and dabbed his mouth with his napkin. "It's a wonderful old Shaker melody, I think. I have to say I'm with Weenie on this one. The guy who wrote the lyrics, whoever he was, was for sure talking about Jesus."

"Ha!" Weenie exclaimed triumphantly, giving Jimmy an elbow.

"But," Ray continued, "and this is just my own view, while Jesus may be the dance man, I think the song is more about us than him."

"What do you mean?" Daphne asked.

Ray answered, "I just think for us, for everyone, the Lord of the Dance can be whoever or whatever we want him to be. We all have our own idea of the Dance Man, but the ideas are on the inside. On the outside, the Dance Man, if there is one, is way, way beyond our knowing. For me, what really matters in life is that we all learn to dance. And to sing and to love life and love one another."

The yellow-orange flames in the fireplace flickered and crackled as Ray's little audience contemplated what Ray had said. Mort, seemingly mesmerized, stared into the fire. "Interesting," he said, hardly above a whisper.

Chapter 25

WEENIE AND MORT SAT IN front of Perry Blevins' big mahogany desk. The lawyer offered coffee which they both accepted. Blevins leaned forward and pressed a button on a little black box in front of him. "Shirley, would you bring in some coffee for our guests, please?" He sat back, clasped his hands together in front of him and said, "Well, then, shall we start?"

"Sure," Weenie said.

"First, let me say that my practice is exclusively wills and estate planning, and I have to tell you that working with your aunt has been one of my most unusual cases."

Mort and Weenie glanced at each other and chuckled. "What a shock," Mort said.

Shirley entered with a tray of coffee, cream and sugar and departed, closing the door behind her.

Blevins resumed. "So let me give you both a little background here. One day last summer, Maggie and her friend, Miss Jamison, showed up here unannounced and said that Miss Paxton wanted to make out a will. So Shirley scheduled an appointment and the two of them came back the following week. We sat and talked. Maggie was a little vague, a little unsure what she wanted. I offered to make some notes of her wishes, if she would share them, and then prepare a rough draft of a will for her review. She said she didn't really trust lawyers and, looking at my computer, said she wasn't so sure about 'those machines.' Anyway, she said she wanted to write her will herself which, of course, is her right, but it did make me wonder why she had come to see me. I then suggested she write what she wanted and bring the text back here and allow me to review it."

The Boozer siblings quietly enjoyed their coffees while listening to the tale.

"Well," Blevins continued, "the two of them showed up a third time and asked where Maggie could sit and write her will. I put them in the conference room. An hour later, they surfaced, and Maggie handed me what she had written. I reviewed it and suggested some changes to clarify the document, all of which she rejected. I feel a little badly that I couldn't be of much help, but you know, your aunt is—was—a bit stubborn."

"Oh, yes, just a tiny bit," Weenie chuckled. Mort rolled his eyes.

"Anyway," Blevins said, "here it is. Take a look."

He slid a single sheet of yellow lined paper across his desk. Weenie took the paper and held it so she and Mort could read it together. The document, in Maggie's small, jerky handwriting, read:

To anybody who needs to know,

When I pass on, here is what I want to happen. I have some money and other stuff in the bank and I want it to go to Jonah and Genia. Jonah has been good to me for lots of years and I want him to have it. Now, the house. Roweena has been good to me too and so when I am gone, she gets the house and the furniture. About the other fella there. If Roweena wants to split the house with him, it's OK with me. But it's up to her.

So I think that is everything. So long.

Magnolia B. Paxton

PS Take care of Seymour please.

Mort and Weenie read the will a second time. When they finished, Blevins shuffled a few papers on his desk and said, "So there you have it. You can see she was pretty vague on a couple of things. If anyone ever challenged that will by itself, it could be a problem. Because of that, I prepared a codicil."

"A what?" Mort asked.

"A codicil," Blevins said. "It's like an amendment that clarifies a few things."

"Such as?" Weenie asked.

"Such as where she writes 'that fella', I specify that she is referring to Mortimer Boozer, Jr. We also specified that 'money and other stuff' encompasses all financial holdings, including but not necessarily limited to, stocks, bonds, mutual funds and cash. We also added Jonah's last name and his wife's full name and your full name, Roweena. Things like that. Anyway, Maggie approved the amendment and signed it, her distrust of lawyers notwithstanding. I'm going to give you, Roweena, copies of the will, the codicil and all other relevant documents."

"Me?" Weenie asked. "Is that because I'm the executioner?"

"You're the executor," Blevins corrected.

"Yes, sorry," Weenie said, her face turning red. "Executor. What exactly does that mean?"

Blevins leaned forward over his desk. "It means you are to execute, that is, carry out, the wishes of the deceased as stated in the will."

"Oh."

"This is a pretty straight forward will," Blevins said. "Basically, you just need to make sure Maggie's bank holdings go to Jonah, that the deed of trust for the house is formally transferred to you. Don't worry. I can help you with all that."

"Well, thanks," Weenie said, "that's a relief."

"Oh, I almost forgot one thing," Blevins said. "One day not too long ago, Maggie and her friend stopped by the office again when I was out. Maggie asked if she could add one small thing to the will. Shirley got the will and witnessed the add-on.

Mort and Weenie waited expectantly.

"It was that PS about Seymour." Blevins looked first at Weenie, then at Mort. "Do either of you know a Seymour, or do you have a last name?"

"Yes, we both know Seymour and, no, he doesn't have a last name," Mort said.

"No last name?" Blevins asked.

"But he does have one eye, four legs and long tail," Weenie said. "Not to worry. We will take good care of ol' Seymour."

🙟🙝

Outside the lawyer's office, Weenie and Mort walked to the car with Weenie, brow furrowed, tightly clutching the manila folder with the will and associated papers. Weenie asked Mort, "So what do we do now?"

As Mort opened the car door for her, he replied, "Don't ask me. You're the executioner."

Chapter 26

P EOPLE SAY TIME FLIES. HOWEVER, in south Alabama it usually
just soldiers on. But the years after Maggie's demise were witness
to many changes around the Boozer homestead and seemed to
move along at a pretty brisk clip.

Another Thanksgiving Day in Collier Bluff. This one the fifth since
Maggie's passing, dawned cool and bright. Not long after the funeral,
Weenie and Mort had decided to move the garden bench out near the
river. It was now getting on to late afternoon. Weenie and Jimmy were
sitting together on the bench enjoying a light November breeze off the
river. Three days earlier, Seymour had loped down toward the Monacoosa
and simply disappeared. Weenie and Jimmy had searched for him for an
entire day, finally concluding that some varmint had brought him to his
end. Maggie had taken Seymour in as a stray and so no one knew his age,
but he was well into his teens. He had been a lucky dog for sure, leading
a very lazy, comfortable life.

Jimmy's arm was now stretched out straight along the back of the
bench behind Weenie. He said to her, "Maybe we should head back in
and help the others a little."

Weenie's response was sharp and immediate. "Hell no! This is the first
family dinner I can remember that I'm not spending half the night and all
day in the kitchen, and I'm gonna enjoy it."

Jimmy patted her shoulder. "I suppose you're right," he said.

"Darn right, I'm right."

Dabney and Lila Ann had volunteered to prepare the meal, and Ray and Mort were inside helping. Jimmy and Weenie sat for a while watching Aaron the heron strut his stuff along the far bank. Weenie looked out past the big bird to the marsh grass and then farther out to the orange sun low on the horizon. "Been almost five years, hasn't it, since Maggie passed," she said.

"I guess it has been that long," Jimmy said. "Sure been a lot of things changed since then, huh?"

Weenie chuckled. "Boy, I'll say."

And indeed, now a half decade later, things were quite rearranged. All told, it was sort of a Dixie version of *Three Weddings and a Funeral*. After the Christmas the year Maggie died, Jane Ellen went downhill rapidly and was gone before spring. At the gravesite, Jimmy read a passage from his Uncle Steeney's diary. It was his entry from Easter Sunday, 1956:

Christ is risen today. Maybe. If so, that sure would be nice; but I've decided it's a waste of time to worry about what is or what isn't. The universe is just what it is, and we are part of it. If we can live in the present as much as we can, be good to each other and do the best we can, then I think things maybe will take care of themselves.

When Jimmy finished reading, he looked up and said, "I really like that, and so did Jane Ellen. She tried to live in the present. She was good to other people, especially me, and she did the best she could."

After they buried her—with her red wig on—Weenie had reached out to Jimmy to provide comfort and solace. As the spring of that year blossomed into summer, their time together slowly turned into a warm friendship, then to affection and, by Labor Day, to romance. They were married the following winter at the First Baptist Church of Collier Bluff. After a brief reception, organized by Miss Mavis and the ladies of the Collier Bluff Bible Study, Jimmy whisked his bride away in his red truck trailering the outboard, with Seymour happily standing lookout at the bow. Before merging on to the interstate toward the Gulf, Jimmy pulled over and brought Seymour into the cab and settled him, wedged him actually, between himself and his bride who was still in her wedding dress. After a memorable, but rather unromantic drive south, Weenie was further treated to an even more memorable boat ride out to Dauphin Island amidst spitting rain, white caps and twenty knot winds.

Following three days and two nights on the island, the honeymooners returned to Collier Bluff. Jimmy put his own house up for sale and moved into the old Boozer home. Weenie had exercised her option of offering half the house to Mort, but by the time of the wedding, Mort was spending most of his time in Georgia with Lila Ann.

Wedding number two took place in Atlanta a few months later. By placing a single phone call to Jimmy, Mort was able to make all the necessary arrangements, free of any creativity on his part, for his own honeymoon. After their wedding and a large, drawn out dinner reception, Mort and Lila Ann drove to Collier Bluff, borrowed Jimmy's red truck and boat, continued to the Gulf of Mexico, motored by sea to Dauphin Island and stayed where Weenie and Jimmy had stayed. Five days later, they returned to Atlanta and began their married life in Lila Ann's stately home in the toney Buckhead section of town.

Meanwhile, Dabney and the good priest had discovered that St. Louis was indeed on the way to Memphis and that the two cities were not really that far apart. Unbeknownst to anyone in Alabama, a Dixie *Tale of Two Cities* was developing with Dabney and Father Ray driving to see one another with increasing frequency.

It was on a lovely south Alabama spring day when Jimmy stepped out on the front veranda of the old house, now his house, and stooped to retrieve the day's mail. He settled into a white wicker chair and casually scanned the magazines and envelopes. Weenie came out holding a lunch tray laden with two chicken salad sandwiches, a bowl of grapes and two tall glasses of sweet tea. She placed their lunch on the table before them. She sat in her own wicker chair next to Jimmy and studied the pile of mail on Jimmy's lap. "Anything interesting there?" she asked.

"Maybe," Jimmy said, handing her an envelope. "Something from Memphis."

"Oh," Weenie said, examining the letter. "Curious."

She opened it and began to read. She moved the letter to one hand, drawing her free hand to her mouth. "Oh God!" she gasped, "Dabney, you daffy dame, what have you done?"

159

"What?" Jimmy asked.

Weenie handed the correspondence to her new husband, threw her head back and closed her eyes. While Jimmy read, Weenie gulped half her ice tea, went into the living room, topped her glass off with bourbon and reemerged, quite shaken, on the porch.

What Jimmy was reading was not a letter. It was an invitation.

Y'all Come!
Dabney Boozer Sweeney and Raymond Reilly
Cordially invite you to their Wedding
At four o'clock in the Afternoon
June First
Tyler Park by the Mississippi River
Memphis, Tennessee
Barbeque Reception following the Ceremony
at the Rendezvous

Jimmy read the invitation again. "Is this a joke?" he asked.

"If it were anyone other than my nutty daughter, I might say yes," Weenie sighed, wiping a drip of tea-bourbon from her chin.

"Probably not going to be a Catholic service," Jimmy speculated.

"Ya think?" Weenie snarled, gulping more of her drink.

Jimmy took a large bite of his sandwich and chewed thoughtfully. He swallowed and said, "It's actually kind of nice in a way, don't you think? I mean how often can a brother and sister have their son and daughter marry each other?"

"Oh, yes," Weenie said. "It's very sweet, especially when the groom is a JESUIT PRIEST!"

෴

And so Mort and Lila Ann and Jimmy and Weenie dutifully journeyed to Memphis to witness, as Weenie described it, "the nuptials of a fallen mackerel snapper and ditzy dame".

Their honeymoon, unlike the two earlier ones, had been very carefully planned, was far from Alabama and did not involve any dogs or boats. Instead, ex-Father Ray whisked his blushing bride to the Arizona desert where they participated in An Encounter With The Great I Am That Is The You, a week long new-age program complete with bearded gurus, bongo drums and moonlit meditations. The newlyweds returned to Memphis where they rented a small cottage by the Mississippi river, bought a beagle puppy, and converted to Buddhism.

The past half-decade had brought other changes as well around the old homestead. Contrary to Weenie's confident predictions, Kamikaze Karl finally fell into Mort's trap and tried unsuccessfully to penetrate the kitchen window at high speed. Fortunately for the bird, still of unknown variety, the impact was sufficiently violent to prevent prolonged suffering. Mort took great delight in flinging the deceased bird out to the middle of the Monacoosa, where upon Aaron swooped low and plucked it from the flowing waters. Aaron chewed as he flew, finding the feathery morsel not to his liking. He glided, wings set, and circled back toward the river and drop-bombed Karl in the middle of the white bench.

And there was yet one final development that took place around the old place after Mort had married and decamped to Atlanta. It was on a very steamy July day in Collier Bluff when the ever persistent Charles Lodger once again paid a call at the old homestead. Weenie was at Miss Mavis' that morning studying the Bible with the other ladies. Jimmy responded to the knock at the front door.

"Good morning, sir," the visitor said in a cheery tone. "My name is Charles Lodger. I represent Face to FaceCustom Windows over in Mobile."

Around lunch time, the returning Weenie was greeted by her new husband. "Honey, I have some good news for us. I just arranged to have all our creaky old windows preplaced with brand new ones!"

So now the time had come again for another Thanksgiving dinner at the old house. The sun had just set, when Dabney pushed open the screen door and called out to Weenie and Jimmy. "Hey, y'all. Dinner's on the table. Come and get it."

"Be right there," Weenie called over her shoulder.

Jimmy and Weenie stood and looked across the river for a long minute, basking in the soft glow of the western sky. As they turned toward the house, they heard a rustling and snapping of brush behind them. The rustling continued until the brown head of an animal emerged from the grass. It was Seymour. Jimmy ran to him and dropped to his knees, throwing his arms around his neck. "Hey, you old coot, where the hell have you been?"

Seymour had burrs and scratches in his fur and looked a bit weary, but otherwise seemed little worse for wear. He nuzzled Jimmy and licked his face as Weenie followed and joined the homecoming celebration.

৩৯৫৩

This Thanksgiving dinner was a reunion of sorts, albeit with several previous attendees absent. Maggie, for obvious reasons, was not able to attend, nor was Jane Ellen. Weenie had invited Jonah and Eugenia, but they were also unable to attend as they were out of town. Way out of town.

As part of her duties as executor of the will, Weenie had, of course, informed Jonah of his inheritance and arranged with the bank and lawyer Blevins for the transfer of assets. Miss Maggie, it turned out, had a tidy sum locked away in the First National Bank of Collier Bluff. A very tidy sum. After receiving his inheritance, Jonah continued to look after the old house and the grounds, now for no pay. But he took care of his maintenance work sporting a spanking new pair of dungaree overalls, a new straw hat and a colorful assortment of new checkered handkerchiefs. He had loved Miss Maggie and tried, in memory of her, to be attentive in his caretaking duties. However, given his heavy travel schedule, it was most challenging.

Jonah and Eugenia and Colie had joined that elite circle of Collier Bluff jet setters, the members of which, including the three of them, could be counted on one hand. Since Maggie's passing, they had visited the Grand Canyon and Disneyland in California. They had taken in the best of New Orleans jazz, stayed in the Waldorf Astoria in New York, gone to plays on Broadway and attended a World Series, all seven games. This year, because they had previously arranged to spend Thanksgiving in Cancun, they were obliged to regret Weenie's invitation. Just before departing, however, Jonah had presented Weenie and Jimmy with a large jug of freshly fermented homemade Scuppernong wine.

So it was just the six of them this year sharing the Thanksgiving feast; six who, through the strangest of circumstances, were now three married couples.

Lila Ann gestured toward the side board and said, "Our Tom Turkey and all the fixings are ready for you. Grab your plates and get in line."

Minutes later, they were all back in their seats facing full plates of turkey, stuffing, grilled ochre, mashed potatoes and ambrosia.

The spiritual inclinations of the six had shifted, not entirely, but to a large extent, over the past five years. God danced and darted among them, taking on various guises, playing hide and seek. Weenie's faith, alone within the group, had remained constant with her god, Jesus, her Rock and her Redeemer. Lila Ann's god was also Jesus, but her Jesus was more of a social friend with whom she and her cultured Buckhead neighbors associated. Jimmy and God had quietly grown apart since Jane Ellen's death. It was not that Jimmy had become an atheist, or even an agnostic, but rather that he had simply abandoned any outreach, jocular or serious, to the Big Guy. Mort, in the meantime, following his nuptials, started going to church with Lila Ann on a regular basis, unless his attendance interfered with fishing or some other high priority activity. Mort's god often appeared as a menacing black cloud and he still shuddered at the sound of thunder. So he attended church just often enough to cover his bets on eternity. Besides, while deep down inside, he never became convinced Jesus was divine, he continued to regard Him as an all-around good guy.

Ray and Dabney, on the other hand, had become very enthused with their new found spiritual path. Their god was, well, hard to describe. The All-in-All? The Great Void? Maybe, the Eternal Now. They had acquired little Buddha statues and some nice smelling incense candles. When visiting Collier Bluff, they would often sit on Maggie's white bench out by the river, palms open, eyes closed, chanting 'oooohhmmm.'

ᏳᏒᏇ

The wonderful aroma of turkey and hot stuffing filled the house. Mort held his knife and fork, poised to dig in. Weenie gathered everyone's attention, stopping Mort in mid-cut. "I know we have diverse faiths now among us here, but I would like to say grace before we eat," Weenie said. "Now three of us are Christians here...."

"Two and a half," Lila Ann said, glancing at Mort.

"Well, that's still a plurality," Weenie said, "so I think I can say a grace here in my own house and mention Jesus."

"No problem here," Ray chirped.

"Go for it, Mom," Dabney said with a fist pump into the air.

Five of the six present bowed their heads. Mort gazed out the big bay window, sensing something odd. He couldn't put his finger on it. The view of the great outdoors seemed somehow sharper, more immediate. He sensed something greater than himself. It was as if he was peering sort of face-to-face at a great mystery. Joining the rest, he closed his eyes and bowed his head. Weenie intoned, "Lord, we thank you for bringing us together on this special day. We thank You for our health and for the banquet before us."

Mort's right hand moved stealthily toward his fork, but halted in mid-reach as his sister continued, "And we thank our dear Aunt Maggie for providing us with this wonderful old home for us to enjoy. And I want to specifically thank my brother for moving out of state long enough to finally give us a decent Scuppernong yield to provide this delicious Vin de Jonah."

Folks quietly chuckled. Mort now touched his fork.

"And now," Weenie said with a cheery voice, lifting her head and raising her glass, "a toast to the Dance Man!"

Mort raised high his glass. "May he dance forever!"

Jimmy, Dabney, Lila and Ray joined in, although each clueless as to who or what they were toasting

As much as Mort was salivating over his plate, he felt compelled to offer a few words of his own. He pushed his chair back and stood, holding his glass of Vin de Jonah. "I would like to offer my own toast here." He paused for dramatic effect and said, "A toast to our family, the esteemed and distinguished clan of the Boozers of Alabama. To that noble Southern family and to those of you, Jimmy and Lila Ann, who by the grace of God, were lucky enough to marry into it!"

"Hear, hear!" all chimed.

And God, whoever or whatever He is, at that moment was smiling down on Collier Bluff, Alabama, and graced them all. For a brief time, the room was silent while everyone sipped their wine. Silent that is, except for Seymour's rhythmic snoring under the table.